*STAR TREK 23:*
# THE COVENANT
# OF THE CROWN

# *STAR TREK* NOVELS

# *STAR TREK: THE NEXT GENERATION* NOVELS

# *STAR TREK* GIANT NOVELS

A *STAR TREK*®
NOVEL

# THE COVENANT
# OF THE CROWN
## HOWARD WEINSTEIN

## TITAN BOOKS
### LONDON

*STAR TREK* 23: THE COVENANT OF THE CROWN
ISBN 1 85286 131 2

Published by
Titan Books Ltd
58 St Giles High St
London WC2H 8LH

First Titan Edition May 1989
10  9  8  7  6  5  4  3  2  1

British edition by arrangement with Pocket Books, a division of
Simon & Schuster, Inc., Under Exclusive License from
Paramount Pictures Corporation, The Trademark Owner.

Printed and bound in Great Britain by Cox and Wyman Ltd,
Reading, Berkshire.

*For Kimberly*

*A hope for a world
where there'll always be
some who are willing to
tilt at windmills*

*And in memory of
Harry Chapin*

*Who started to make
that hope a reality*

# Author's Notes

Quite a bit has happened in the world of *Star Trek* since I began writing this novel. The major event, of course, was *Star Trek: The Motion Picture.* After all the years of anticipation, *any* movie would have been hard-pressed to live up to our expectations. If *ST: TMP* fell short in some areas, it also excelled in others. (I'll never forget the feeling of delight shared with Kirk when he—and we—saw the new *Enterprise* for the first time, cradled in its drydock.)

Critics didn't like the movie much—but it still went on to become one of the biggest-grossing movies in Hollywood history. It certainly wasn't perfect, and fan enthusiasm has declined some since then, but the essence of what made us love *Star Trek* before is still there.

That thought hit me recently while watching a rare prime-time rerun. There's something about wee-morning or late-afternoon air times that demeans the repeats of great old TV series. On this night, however, "The Ultimate Computer" (one of my favorites) had a renewed glory, riding head-to-head with network competition, just like the old days. And it didn't seem like a fourteen-year-old rerun. The writing and acting, the look and *feel* of the show were as fresh and crisp and real as any series currently on the air.

And that's why *Star Trek* has survived—and why it will continue to survive. Gene Roddenberry did a wonderful job of creation, and we have done a wonderful job of being loyal, creative, and critical fans. We managed to keep *Star Trek* alive through the years of struggling to bring it back, and through whatever disappointments the movie or any of the other books may have caused.

It's important to remember that every piece of *Star Trek* is just that—*a part of a whole*—and some parts are bound to be better than others. But none of the lesser stories or TV episodes can diminish the sterling quality of the good ones.

The sum of *Star Trek*'s parts is and always will be impressive. It has touched too many people's lives in too many important ways to be any less. *Star Trek* has earned its niche of honor in entertainment and science-fiction history. Be proud that you're a fan.

I owe a lot to Gene Roddenberry. Though I've only met him once (at a convention in Washington, D.C., where he graciously bought me a drink), in many ways, he's changed my life.

After all, it was his TV series that made me think about being a writer (you know the show—the one with the guy with the pointed ears).

Some random memories. . . . When I used to rush to watch the reruns every night during high school, my mother would warn: "The world doesn't revolve around *Star Trek*." Not the whole world, Mom, but some of it.

On Saturday morning, September 7, 1974, it did—when the second animated season kicked off with "The Pirates of Orion" and thirty people and one dog crammed into my college dorm room to watch, and everyone applauded (except the dog) when the screen flashed "Written by . . ."

That turned out to be a great way to impress a girl on a first date the night before: "Gee, if you're not doing anything tomorrow morning," I said shyly, "would you like to come over and watch my TV show?" That really happened.

Since then, I've been a guest at more than a dozen *Star Trek* conventions, talked at libraries and schools, and had a lot of fun. (I'm still available for all these things. . . .)

I've gotten to meet many of *Star Trek*'s cast members, found out they're real people with ups and downs, and marveled at the way they can patiently and consistently charm hordes of eager fans.

Most of all, I've made so many friends through *Star*

9

*Trek*, many of whom also want to be writers. There's been a lot of mutual encouragement along the way.

More than a few people deserve special thanks. I wish I could mention them all, but here are some:

The Febcon and August Party Committees, for making me feel at home and bringing an outsider in; to Alina Chu and Bob Greenberger, for the "fan club" and friendship (and Bob's editorial help); to Bonnie MacRitchie, for helpful comments when this was just a wee, scribbled outline; to Frank Pellegrino, whose freshly hatched Honda gave its back bumper that I might shop for shirts in Virginia when all mine were left in New York; to Lynne Perry and the New York Diabetes Association, for the days off to write all this; to Allan Asherman, for commiseration; and Linda Deneroff for defending the cause of the semi-colon . . .

. . . Also to David Gerrold, for being a buddy and treating me like a real writer, and for contributing this book's introduction; to my former apartment mate, Joel Pineles, whose slight midriff bulge (he is now svelte) suggested Chekov's dilemma herein; to T. J. Burnside, for being an extra-special friend; to Cindi Casby, for love and encouragement even when I didn't deserve them . . .

. . . And to my parents, who *didn't* pack me off to law or medical school. Not that there's anything wrong with being a doctor or a lawyer, but I'd rather be a writer. Hope you're not disappointed, Mom and Dad.

Last, I'd like to note that this is really for all the fellow-fans I've met, for the ones who've told me what they liked or didn't like about past *Star Trek* novels and stories. I hope you all enjoy *this* one—let me know by writing to me c/o Pocket Books Inc., 1230 Avenue of the Americas, New York, New York 10020.

HOWARD WEINSTEIN

January, 1981

# Introduction

I told Howard that he would have been better off if he had had his mother write this introduction. She would have told you what a fine boy he is, intelligent, bright, alert, clean, respectful of his parents, and a perfect catch for some nice young Jewish girl. And she would have been able to say it all with a straight face.

Me, the best I can tell you is that Howard Weinstein is a credit to his species. Whatever that is.

I think my first realization that Howard Weinstein was a writer to be reckoned with occurred at the banquet of a *Star Trek* convention, when the Howard Weinstein monks, a group of neo-Hare Krishna worshipers, came marching into the room, all dressed in white robes (bedsheets, I think), threading their way through the tables of astonished banqueteers, chanting a strangely compelling mantra —the rhythm of which was frequently punctuated by the sound of the worshipers slapping themselves in the forehead with a Howard Weinstein book. It was at that moment I wished that Howard Weinstein had authored *War and Peace*.

I am not making this up.

Howard Weinstein was born on September 16, 1954. This is exactly two hundred and sixty-two years (to the day) after eighty-year-old Giles Corey, charged with witchcraft, was crushed to death in Salem, Massachusetts. I do not suggest that there is any connection between these two events. The facts speak for themselves. Also on September 16 (but of unknown year), Klaatu and Gort arrived/will arive in Washington, D.C. (Had

Howard Weinstein been considerate enough to be born two days earlier, I could have noted that it was exactly two years to the day before the first successful prefrontal lobotomy was performed, and done all kinds of wonderful extrapolations on that particular coincidence. As it is, however, there is nothing particularly distinguished about Howard Weinstein's birth, its circumstances, or the day on which it occurred. Which makes it all that much harder to demonstrate the portents and signs that herald his arrival as a serious writer in science fiction.)

Howard—Howie, to those of us who know and love him—graduated with a BA in communications from the University of Connecticut in 1975. All historical records of him from the time between his birth and his graduation have been lost (or burned) and there is no proof at all that he really exists, or that the person currently pretending to be Howard Weinstein actually is the one and the same infant who was assigned the name some twenty-one years earlier. For all we know, the current Howard Weinstein is an impostor. A doppelgänger. Perhaps even . . . a clone. (And if so, of *whom*? The real Howard Weinstein perhaps? Where is the *real* Howard Weinstein? Who is covering up?)

This pseudo-Howard person claims that he became hooked on *Star Trek* during its first season and fine-tuned his fannish instincts when the show went into reruns in September of 1969. (At that time he was fifteen years old. For those of you who think that all science-fiction writers are one step removed from gods, let me reassure you that this is not *always* the case. I have it on the best authority that Howard Weinstein—or the person pretending to be him—was just as much a painfully shy, spoiled-brat, four-eyed little acne-pocked bookworm as the rest of us were when we were fifteen. Perhaps even more so. That he later grew out of it is a source of inspiration for all humanity. Have hope. Everybody was fifteen once; but you don't have to be fifteen forever.)

Because there were no more new *Star Trek* stories being written for television, he began writing his own.

For fun.

Let me digress a moment.

Many of those who are writing *Star Trek* novels today

started out writing their own *Star Trek* stories for fun, because there were no more *Star Trek* stories being written for television. Kathleen Sky, Sondra Marshak, Myrna Culbreath, and so on.

These people would all be considered a little . . . well, eccentric, were it not for the fact that there are obviously millions of other people who share their desire for more *Star Trek* stories. (It's a good guess that you are one of those persons. If not, what are you doing reading this book?)

In 1969, *Star Trek* was one of the few moments of hope in the American experience. The rest of it seemed to be drug overdoses, riots, demonstrations, clumsy politics, acts of terrorism, mass murders, tear gas, napalm, and war.

That *Star Trek* continues to be as popular today as it was ten years ago (before we solved all of those problems, remember?) is an indicator that there is *always* a market for hope.

And that is why *Star Trek*—as a dream—is still going strong today.

If nothing else, *Star Trek* is about hope. Hope for the future. Hope for ourselves, for our nation, for our world, for our dreams. Writing *Star Trek* stories is a small part of that hope. It's not just a dream of your favorite TV series; it's a dream of humanity among the stars, willfully choosing to be masters of our own destinies, captains of our own fates.

Sometimes you have to be a little bit crazy—uh, eccentric—to hope in the face of massive adversity.

I noted above that sometimes science-fiction writers—because of their aura of expertise about the future—seem as gods. Not bloody likely. At best we are a lesser breed of hero, because we are the men and women who listen to the future and report back what we hear.

To be heroic is to *dare* to be different. Very often, the hero is a social illiterate. If he were well-integrated into his culture, he would be content; he would have no need to be a hero. That he is not content, that he does not fit in, that he does not accept the circumstance of today, mandates that he look to tomorrow.

Dreamers may be misfits, but we are *proud* misfits.

Dreams are our most important natural resource. They are the source of hope.

End of digression. Now I can talk about Howard Weinstein again.

Howard had a dream.

And what distinguishes each of us is the size of our dreams.

Howard was co-editor of his high-school SF magazine, called *Probe*. He printed his original *Star Trek* short story in it, a piece called "The Pirates of Orion." Two years later, in 1973, NBC decided to try *Star Trek* as an animated revival, so Howard rewrote "Pirates" as a script, having been hooked on the idea of scriptwriting after reading *The Making of Star Trek* way back in 1969. After a rather roundabout, confused jouney that saw the manuscript travel to his agent, to Filmation with D. C. Fontana's name on the envelope (then associate producer of the animated series), to D. C. Fontana, who was no longer with the show by then, who returned it unopened to his agent, who sent it back to Howard and instructed him to mail it to Norm Prescott at Filmation if he read that the show was renewed for a second season, in which case they would then be interested in actually reading it . . . which it was, and he did, and they did, and finally after he rewrote the ending several times (par for the television course), they bought it and "The Pirates of Orion" was the opening episode of the second season, which Howard is quick to point out is the season the show won the Emmy.

One long run-on sentence later, Howard Weinstein—or whoever he really is—had become a *Star Trek* TV writer at the age of nineteen, and as far as anyone has yet determined, he was the youngest person ever to write for the show—taking the title away from yours truly, who had previously held that distinction for having sold "The Trouble with Tribbles" at the wizened age of twenty-three.

I will pass over some of the details of Howard Weinstein's and my friendship, they being of interest only to the morbidly curious. However, I should note that it is a sign of my devotion to Howard (at least, I think it's Howard. Howard, is that you?) that I would interrupt my own writing schedule to take the time to tell you what a marvelous person he is. Suffice it to say that I like him anyway.

This novel that you are holding, *The Covenant of the*

*Crown,* is Howard Weinstein's first novel. (Those monks who were hitting themselves in the forehead with it were obviously time travelers visiting from the future, a sure sign that Howard Weinstein is destined for greater triumphs in the years to come, else why bother?) Howard believes that this publication makes him the only writer from either the original or the animated TV series versions of *Star Trek* to also write a *Star Trek* novel, certainly the youngest to accomplish both. The first part of that distinction, he will be able to claim only until I can finish *my Star Trek* novel (untitled at this writing) and get it turned in.* The second part, he will undoubtedly keep.

Read. Enjoy. Tell friends.

DAVID GERROLD

---

* No, David and I haven't forgotten that Gene Roddenberry has, of course, also written TV and novel episodes of *Star Trek.* Other than the Great Bird of the Galaxy, we're the only ones. —H.W.

# Chapter One

"It's gray, Jim," said Dr. Leonard McCoy. The ship's surgeon stood before the mirror on his office wall, scratching through his thatch of hair as if searching for the cause of some mysterious medical condition.

It was Captain James Kirk's first inkling that the birthday party might be a major mistake.

At times, Kirk had the feeling the whole universe was aligned against him. There were the big things, like wars or supernovas, events so obviously out of his control he couldn't take them personally. But when the little plans, best-laid as they might be, also went astray, he had to wonder what he'd done to deserve his fate.

In the grand order of history, his medical officer's birthday might not mean much, but Kirk wanted it to be special. After all, McCoy had no better friend in the galaxy, so the captain was determined not to let the event pass unhonored.

Until he discovered that McCoy himself wanted it to pass not only unhonored, but totally unnoticed.

"Completely gray," McCoy repeated, glowering.

"Oh, come on, Bones. A little silver around the temples is hardly completely gray," Kirk said, a glint of amusement in his eyes as he stood behind McCoy.

McCoy glared at the captain's reflection over his shoulder. "It's not funny, Jim. I'm turning ancient and you're in hysterics."

"You're exaggerating just a bit."

"That," said McCoy tartly, "is also a sign of old age."

His mood failed to improve as he and Kirk stepped out of the turbolift near one of the ship's messes.

"Do you realize how long it's been since anyone's called me 'Lenny' . . . or 'son'?"

"Bones, do you really miss being called 'son'?"

"No. I hated it when I was a kid," McCoy said, pausing as a pretty yeoman came out of the messroom. She smiled at them and disappeared around the curving corridor. "But it was a whole lot nicer when two-thirds of the ladies on board weren't young enough to be my daughters. There's only one solution—swear off birthdays altogether. Just ignore them."

*Oops,* Kirk thought as they entered to eat. Should he scrap the birthday plans? The invitations he'd had posted with the duty notices, appearing on everyone's cabin computer screen but McCoy's . . . the food he'd ordered specially programmed, with threats against anyone who might let the secret slip. . . . Cancel a potentially great surprise party just because the man whose birthday it was wanted no part of it?

Certainly not. If McCoy wanted to be a wet blanket, so be it. Most birthday parties on board the USS *Enterprise* were small affairs, with only the closest friends of the guest of honor. But this was to be a rare, shipwide gathering; after all, even the youngest crew members had come to regard the doctor as a crotchety, eccentric uncle, the kind who scolded you as a kid and then passed you a piece of candy when your mother wasn't looking. Everyone knew McCoy's caring went far deeper than mere professional responsibility.

And Kirk knew that *mutiny* was a distinct possibility if he canceled the whole idea after all the plans had been made and anticipation built. If he needed a last word to allay his fears, Chief Engineer Montgomery Scott was there to offer it, with that touch of common-sense insight he often displayed—whenever he could be coaxed to look away from his engines.

"Put McCoy in a room with the ladies, plenty o' good drink, some fine food, and a bit o' the singin'," said Scott, "and he'll snap right out o' whatever's ailin' him."

Later, Kirk gave the signal on schedule. In twos and threes, off-duty crewmen headed for the large rec room on deck seven. The tough part remained for Kirk himself to master—getting McCoy to stop counting gray hairs long enough to attend the celebration.

"Let's go, Bones," Kirk said to the inert body curled on McCoy's bunk.

"Let me lie in the dark. Maybe I'll stop getting older," McCoy sighed. "If I had leaves, at least I'd stop photosynthesizing."

"You're a doctor, not a plant," Kirk said, grunting as he grabbed McCoy's arm and pulled him to a sitting position. He felt slightly foolish. "Come on. I have no intention of carrying you."

"Where aren't you carrying me?"

"To the rec room."

McCoy tried to slump back into his fetal position, but Kirk held his arm. "Aww, leave me alone, Jim. What am I going to do in the rec room in this state of mind?"

"You're going to snap out of it, that's what. I've planned a chance for you to engage in one of your favorite pastimes—baiting Spock while I play chess with him."

McCoy let out a long slow sigh, like a deflating tire. "Well, when you put it that way." He got to his feet and followed Kirk out. McCoy's glumness made the excursion to deck seven somewhat less cheery than a stroll to the gallows, and Kirk suppressed the urge to go back.

They turned into the rec room and the doors slid open to reveal a completely dark cavern. Kirk pushed his friend forward and the lights suddenly flashed on, strobing in red, blue, yellow and white. Without uttering a sound, McCoy jumped back at least three feet, landing squarely on Kirk's toe. The hidden crowd of crewmen popped up from behind tables and planters, shouting, "Happy birthday, McCoy!"

Braced for a look that might kill, Captain Kirk turned to the doctor. McCoy's eyes were glazed with shock. The shouts gave way to applause and laughter, and a lovely lieutenant from the medical staff placed a drink—and herself—in McCoy's hand. Finally, he allowed himself to be drawn into the festivities—but not before he shot a grinning glance back at Kirk. "Jim, I'll get you for this!"

Kirk chuckled and found himself next to his engineer. "I guess you were right, Scotty."

"Well, it's not just engines I know, sir," Scott said, his brow furrowed in false modesty. "The only problem I

can see is, he'll want one o' these every time he feels old.
Come t' think of it, sir . . . I'm feelin' a wee bit old m'self."

Crew members swarmed around the long tables of
cake, hors d'oeuvres, and drinks, and the first trays were
picked clean in no time at all. Chekov poked mournfully
at a nearly microscopic piece of cake with his fork while
Dr. Christine Chapel and Lieutenant Commanders Uhura
and Sulu dug into wedges almost too large for their plates.

"Mmmm," Uhura purred. "I didn't think the food syn-
thesizer could make cake like this."

"It *couldn't*," said Christine. "Not till I changed the
programming a bit."

Everyone laughed—except Chekov. Sulu nudged him.
"What's with you?"

"Where's your party face?" said Uhura.

"I have a feeling this *is* his party face," Sulu said wryly.
"You know these gloomy Russians." He slid his fork under a huge hunk of cake and dumped it on the saturnine
security chief's dish.

Chekov promptly dropped it back onto the serving tray
with a strangled cry of frustration. "It's *fattening.*"

"You're still a growing boy," said Uhura. "Since when
are you worried about fattening foods?"

"Since I seem to have put on an extra ten pounds."

"Where? On your toes?"

Chekov shrugged in genuine dismay. "I don't have the
slightest idea. I don't *feel* fat."

"Christine," said Sulu, "is he really ten pounds overweight?"

Christine nibbled her cake with a distinctly guilty countenance. "That's what the scale said. When we get older,
our metabolism changes. You put on weight more easily
and it goes to different places. Let's face it, Chekov,
you're not twenty-two anymore."

"Don't remind me."

The cheery din and clatter of the party promised to
last a whole diurnal cycle. After all, McCoy had insisted
that all duty shifts get a chance to observe a living relic in
the flesh, even if it was a thoroughly soused relic. Kirk
was on his way out to return to the bridge when the ship
suddenly shuddered. It was a barely perceptible tremor
that would go unnoticed by almost anyone on board—
except Kirk or Scott. Both felt the surge of rapid acceleration, and they moved together to the intercom as First

Officer Spock's voice smoothly said, "Captain Kirk, to the bridge, please."

Kirk touched the wall switch. "Kirk here. Did somebody spirit a case of Scotch up there?"

"Negative, sir. All duty personnel must remain sober."

"Then why are you shaking the ship, Spock?"

"Aye, y'must've gone to warp six."

"Warp eight, Mr. Scott."

"Scotty, I'm surprised at you," Kirk said in mock amazement.

"I guess I've had too much t' drink, sir."

"What's going on. Spock?"

There was an instant of hesitation before the Vulcan replied, and Kirk sensed this was no time for joking. "Perhaps you had best report to the bridge, Captain."

"On my way. Kirk out."

The turbolift doors hissed open. Kirk stepped out onto the bridge deck. Spock swiveled in the center seat and stood.

"We have received a Priority One signal from Star Fleet Command, Security Condition Red, ordering us to Star Base Twenty-two by seventeen hundred hours tomorrow. Warp eight is sufficient to ensure arrival by fifteen-forty-five hours. No further information on why our presence is requested so urgently, sir."

"Not even in code, Spock?"

"Negative. The message simply said that you, Dr. Mc-Coy, and I are to report to Fleet Admiral Harrington immediately upon our arrival."

# Chapter Two

"If this mission fails," said Admiral Paul Harrington in his crisp British accent, "the whole of Quadrant J-221 could be in Klingon hands by next year."

"For my next birthday," McCoy whispered to Kirk.

Harrington spun on his heel. "What was that, Doctor?"

"Nothing, sir."

Harrington was a tall man with impeccable posture. He moved with deliberate precision as he paced on the rug, thick and green as a well-kept lawn. But the pacing was not nervous, just smooth, and poised—a reflection of the man's perpetually active mind. He was English to the core, cut from the same cloth that had produced great seamen and officers for over a thousand years. Harrington had already carved a place in Federation annals with his unflappable handling of crises large and small—and Kirk was well aware that they faced another such critical juncture now.

"There is no alternate source of tridenite in the region?" Spock asked.

"None," said Harrington, puffing on a curved ivory pipe.

"Shad provides that ore for twenty or more planets," Kirk said.

"Can't they get energy from something other than tridenite?" McCoy wondered.

They could not, and Kirk knew it. Shad was one of those worlds with the mixed blessing of having something many other planets needed, wanted, and might even kill for—a virtually unlimited supply in its crust of tridenite, an energy ore far cleaner and safer than uranium or any of the other isotopes that had provided abundant though perilous power for many civilizations. Even Earth had gone through its early period of reliance on dangerous radioactive energy sources. Kirk knew his home world was dotted with caverns where nuclear wastes had been buried hundreds of years before—they'd continue emitting deadly particles for thousands of years to come.

But Shad had been spared that. Tridenite had been tailored by nature for producing vast amounts of efficient energy, and the economies and industries of those twenty other planets were built on the assurance of an uninterrupted flow of the ore.

Half those worlds belonged to the Federation, the others were neutral, but all lived in the shadow of the nearby Klingon Empire. Shad, however, was the linchpin, the coveted prize. Take over Shad, cut off the tridenite supply, watch a score of inhabited planets in Quadrant J-221 fall like dominoes, and sweep in to conquer a valuable flank of the United Federation of Planets. That had been the Klingon goal, and they'd pursued it patiently by igniting a civil war on Shad eighteen years earlier.

Kirk rolled the historical details over in his mind. He knew the Shaddan situation as intimately as any officer, bureaucrat, or diplomat, for a simple reason—he'd been there at the war's inception, in command of a Star Fleet advisory detail attached to the Court of King Stevvin. . . .

After five centuries, the Dynasty of Shad had survived longer than most. Now, suddenly, it teetered on the ragged edge of an abyss—and extinction lay ahead. The young Lieutenant Commander James T. Kirk felt it in his bones as he hurried to the palace for his regular late-morning meeting with the King. He arrived early and he paced the castle grounds under a somber, sunless sky, waiting; inside, the King tried to control another rancorous Council meeting.

Twelve Cabinet ministers ringed the solid dark-wood table, which had been hewn from a single mighty tree by Stevvin's ancestor, Keulane the Healer. Keulane had begun the Dynasty, and Stevvin was ready to accept that he was going to preside over its end. He banged the jewel-handled gavel on the table until its echo drowned out the dozen voices arguing at once.

Sudden silence. Broken only by the deep sigh of a King. He leaned heavily on the table, looking no one in the eye as he spoke at last.

"The Council cannot function this way. We must have order." His voice was soft and raspy, speaking a plea, not a command.

"There *is* no order on Shad," said Yon, a pig-faced minister seated at the far end. "Why do you expect it here —*sire?*" His last word was clearly intended as a sarcastic afterthought.

Stevvin formed a retort in his mind, but swallowed it unspoken. He dropped the gavel and started for the brass-trimmed double doors.

"Sire."

This voice reached out and held him for a moment, though his back remained toward the Council. The King knew the respectful tone of First General Haim, the tall, stooped, bald-headed man who had been aide and friend since before Stevvin had ascended to the throne.

"Sire . . . the Council can't act without you."

"It can't act with me, either. If twelve men and women responsible for this world's government can't overcome their differences to reach a goal—even to speak civilly to one another—then our cause is lost."

Shoulders slumped, Stevvin left the room.

The Loyalist Coalition was crumbling, and while the Council quarreled petulantly, territory was being lost steadily to the despotic Mohd Alliance.

The Alliance had learned well the lessons of treachery taught by its patron, the Klingon Empire. Its leaders salivated over the prospect of becoming guard dogs for the Empire, enslaving the free population of Shad and biting hunks out of the Federation's flesh as the Quadrant came under their domination, planet by planet. The Klingons had seeded massive amounts of weaponry and money in the Mohd Alliance, and the crops were nearly ready for harvest.

Lieutenant Commander Kirk found the King sitting alone in the meditation chamber, a velvet robe loose on his gaunt body. At the sound of a footfall on the carpet, Stevvin raised his eyes and smiled. This brash young officer could almost make him believe there was some hope.

But the grim set of Kirk's jaw told him, wordlessly, that hope was out of reach this time.

"I'm sorry, sir," Kirk said quietly. "The Federation Council has decided it can't spare more troops or supplies for support now. They're afraid of trouble in the Talenic Sector, and a half dozen other places. Maybe in the near future, the resolution can be brought up again . . ." His voice trailed off.

"These are indeed troubled times, James. Their answer is what we expected." His face was deeply shadowed in the flickering candlelight. A gentle fragrance of incense wafted around them.

"I tried to tell them with a little more help, we could win," Kirk said, bitterness overflowing.

"Not *we*. It's not your battle, not your world."

Kirk ignored the King's comment. "They don't understand how close the Mohd is to taking Shad and handing it over to the Klingons. They'll wake up one day, and it'll be too late. I've got to make them see—"

Kirk began to pace, but the King stopped him with a firm hand on his shoulder. "No. It's about time for you and your men to leave."

The young officer looked into Stevvin's tired eyes. Words came only after a long moment of hesitation. "Your Highness, I think it's time for you to leave as well."

"This is my world, a world united by my ancestors. They took a hundred battling nations and molded them into one."

"Except the Mohd Province."

Stevvin nodded grimly. "And if the Covenant of Peace is to be broken by those sons of Hell, then I have to stay to see it happen. When I meet Keulane and my other fathers in the next life, I want them to know I stayed till the end."

Kirk's office was high up in a drafty, dark-stone castle that had once served as a Shaddan monastery. The windows were too small and close to the vaulted ceiling to let in much light. He paced as he waited for a pot of chowder to warm up in the little infrared burner on his desk.

In his year on Shad, Kirk had become close to the old King, and he shared the anguish that Stevvin felt now. In the days before battle losses had become daily events, they'd often spent soft summer evenings on the palace balcony, sipping fruitwine, discussing everything from poetry to history, from battle tactics to bawdy Shaddan tales. When the twin moons set in the coolness of dawn, the two men would more than likely still be out there as witnesses to the night's end.

Kirk was just a young line officer, commanding a force of a hundred men; Stevvin was nearing old age and ruled a planet of a hundred *million* people. But still they'd bridged the gap with friendship, sharing respect and affection.

And if anything tore Kirk apart now more than his own helplessness, it was having to watch a good and gentle King see his planet weakened by a civil war he was powerless to end.

Kirk sipped a steaming spoonful of the native sea chowder. A fresh-faced ensign entered the open door and set a dispatch cassette on the desk.

"It's from the mountain front, sir. It's . . . it's not good news."

Placing the tape in the viewer, Kirk scowled and watched the image of a map as a field commander's flat voice told him what he prayed he'd never hear. The Mohd's artillery had cut Loyalist defense lines and the enemy was advancing on the King's capital city. There was no time to waste.


"I don't care how you do it," Kirk snapped. "Shake a shuttle loose and have it on the palace lawn by fifteen hundred hours. I'll worry about how we get it out of the capital and into space."

He punched the communicator panel button, shutting it off. He rubbed his eyes, stood, and headed down the monastery's ancient stone steps. His feet automatically followed the path across the cobblestoned city square to the palace, looming over the narrow streets from its hillside perch. Kirk's mind wandered to thoughts of the irony of Stevvin's fate.

After five centuries of stability, the Shaddan people, rulers included, had been bred to believe in lasting peace and security. It had become as natural to them as logic had to Vulcans. But it was false security, for under the blanket of unity and progress a sore festered deep in the heart of the Mohd Province, whose warrior people fancied themselves slighted with an unequal share of the planet's wealth. Since ancient times, the Mohd nomads had ranged far to fight any population that accepted their challenge. To them, the peace forged by Keulane and his successors was an affliction, and they swore never to accept it.

Klingon agents had recognized blood brothers in this province of restless warriors, and prodded them to seek out dissent elsewhere on Shad, nurture it, probe the soft underbelly of the old dynasty—and slash it with a lightning stroke of rebellion.

Lieutenant Commander Kirk grudgingly marveled at the Klingons' simple view of the order of things—that discord was ever-present and with the proper encouragement could be made to flare into open war. The status quo was of no use—the Empire could only gain by taking what belonged to someone else. Victory meant advance—loss only that they were back to their starting point. The Klingons truly lived by the adage *Nothing ventured, nothing gained.*

And their Shaddan campaign certainly represented an effective venture. The government under King Stevvin had misjudged the strength of the dark forces in the Mohd Province, unaware that massive clandestine Klingon support in weapons and supplies had created a bristling war machine. So had the Federation miscalculated, perhaps because no Klingon troops were present. Never before had the Empire flexed such power *in absentia;* meanwhile, other trouble spots needed tending, and Kirk knew that the Star Fleet aid he had brought was too little, too late.

Stevvin had held one goal above all others—to keep production and shipment of tridenite ore going. Because Shad had never developed space flight, foreign freighters had to transport the ore to other worlds. As long as Loyalist forces could guard the loading stations against Mohd artillery, tridenite could move and the Klingon grand design remain unfulfilled. So far, he had won that battle—but perhaps at cost of losing the whole war.

And now the Mohd battalions were marching on the capital. Shipping would soon cease. The Dynasty would be strangled; the King and his family would be among the first killed when enemy troops reached the city. Kirk now had one last task before he could order a retreat of his own men—to convince Stevvin to allow Star Fleet to help him escape into exile.

Just outside the brick palace rampart, the young aide from his office caught up to Kirk, a handwritten communique clutched in his fist. His face was flushed—he'd run all the way.

"Sir, this came in just after you left."

Kirk took the paper and prepared himself for a quick glance at another report of negative battle news. He stopped short when he saw it was a message from the Federation Council.

"Why didn't you call me by communicator, Ensign?"

"I didn't want to risk being picked up by Mohd surveillance, sir. The message came in on scramble." He stood at ease as his commander read the page. The Federation had reviewed Kirk's final reports and changed their conclusion—additional military assistance was on its way.

"I had lost all faith," Stevvin confessed.

"They've decided Shad *is* worth fighting for, sir. If this new support is enough to turn it all around—and I think it will be—we want you to be safe," Kirk said.

"But not on Shad," Stevvin said with a half-smile.

"It would only be temporary. A matter of months at most. We'll bring you back here as soon as your safety can be assured."

The King closed his eyes. "What about the safety of our soldiers, and their wives and children? How can that be guaranteed? They can't go into exile."

"Sir, you aren't just another soldier."

"No . . . I suppose not."

Kirk's voice took on an impatient edge. "You're the dynastic ruler of Shad. You lead the religion of your people, you're their rallying point. Without you, there *is* no Shad."

"Let's not forget, there hasn't been much *with* me, either."

"Then think about your wife and daughter, about their safety. Your daughter is Shad's next Queen."

The King finally relented. The shuttlecraft arrived on time and Kirk took over the pilot's seat. Since Shad completely lacked manned flying machines, planetary weapons included no refined antiaircraft capability. Mohd gunners did their best to shoot down the shuttle with large-target missiles when it was detected attempting to reach planet orbit.

Shuttles were never intended for deft evasive motion, and this one groaned in protest as Kirk urged it on a spiral course up toward space. But if they weren't agile, the little ships were sturdy, and Kirk was sure this one would hold together and do what was asked of it. He threaded his way out of missile range and brought the King and his young wife, their five-year-old daughter Kailyn, and four servants within transporter range of the *Normandy*, itself waiting far out of the orbital combat zone around Shad. The destroyer would spirit them to a new home, just until the Loyalists could struggle back and hold the Mohd Alliance in check. . . .

Eighteen years had passed since James Kirk had said farewell to the King and his family, since he'd watched them disappear in the sparkle of the *Normandy*'s transporter. Still, the battle on Shad dragged on, neither side able to muster the last push to victory.

The Organian Peace Treaty had prevented wholesale intervention on either side. If they tried it, the pure-energy beings from that enigmatic guardian world would effectively disarm both forces, on Shad and throughout the galaxy, no matter where or whom they fought. Neither the Federation nor the Empire wanted to risk total galactic immobilization, so they had to be satisfied with simply supplying weapons and hoping for the best. Like a pair of exhausted warriors, the enemies slugged it out with increasingly weary blows.

But, finally, the tide had turned—long after Kirk's expectation. "The Loyalist coalition," said Admiral Harrington, "is on the verge of breaking the back of the Mohd Alliance."

McCoy snorted. "After all this time? What could be left to fight over?"

"More than you might think," Harrington said, exhaling a pair of smoke rings. "Don't forget, this was no nuclear holocaust there. It was a war of quite conventional means, almost primitive. Neither we nor the Klingons wanted to destroy the world we were hoping to take."

"How civilized of us," McCoy said, frowning.

"The point, gentlemen, is that the coalition is also on the verge of destroying itself with internal bickering."

Kirk shook his head sadly. "They haven't even won, and they're trying to divide the spoils."

"That's about the size of it, Captain. The only hope for restoring some semblance of unity, as we see it, is to return the one symbol to which all our Loyalist factions owe allegiance."

Spock raised an eyebrow. "The royal family?"

"Precisely, Commander."

"They're still alive," Kirk said, almost to himself.

"The King and his daughter are. The wife died some years back, not long after the exile began. It's not a pretty planet they went to."

Kirk closed his eyes for a moment, a private memory of Lady Meya's ready smile and warmth. And now the child and the King had lived to return, while she had not.

"Our agents have contacted the King," Harrington continued. "He may be very old, but he's anxious to return. He believes as we do that the presence of the royal family will hold the Loyalists together, allow them to beat down the Mohd Alliance once and for all, and send the Klingons packing. Actually, it's quite simple, gentlemen. Secure Shad and we secure the quadrant. Lose Shad, and you know the consequences."

"Admiral," said Spock, "the *Enterprise* was assigned to another sector. Star Fleet records indicate three other starships patrolling in this vicinity with no pressing assignments. Why were we given this mission?"

Kirk smiled inwardly—Spock was applying the same precision of reason to Harrington as he did to his own captain.

The admiral clasped his hands behind his back and faced them, chewing on his pipe stem for a moment. "Because King Stevvin trusts only one man in the whole of Star Fleet to take him safely back to Shad—Captain James Kirk. Therefore, gentlemen, the mission is yours."

# Chapter Three

PERSONAL LOG—STAR DATE 7815.3—We've arrived
and entered orbit around Orand, and it's hard to believe I'm going to see King Stevvin again after all
these years. On the one hand, I feel like a long-
graduated student going back to visit a favorite
teacher—and that makes me happy.

But I also feel a little like a jailer going down to
release a prisoner, and that makes me feel guilty. I
know the King would've stayed on Shad had it been
up to him, and who's to say he would have
been wrong? After all this time, I just don't know.
Even if he doesn't think eighteen years were stolen
from him, I do—and I'm the one who convinced him
to leave.

I'm anxious to see this mission succeed, to restore
the King to his rightful place. Spock would call it illogical—and maybe he's right . . . but even though I
know those lost years can never be restored, this mission gives me a chance to make up for at least some
of what was taken from my old friend. Politics and
diplomacy be damned—I have to admit my motivation is much more emotional than rational.

"He's not going to make it, Jim." McCoy's face made
the words unnecessary, but he said them anyway, gently.

Kirk stared at the tile floor, cool and shiny in this
house where King Stevvin had spent the past eighteen
years of his life—waiting. And now McCoy had confirmed
what Kirk had feared, that they were indeed the final

years in Stevvin's life—the King was going to die before
he could see his home planet reunited.

"Can I talk to him?" Kirk asked.

"He's sleeping now. In a little while." McCoy shrugged,
feeling useless. "Want to take a walk?"

"Yeah, Bones. Alone."

Spock and McCoy let him go without a word.

Kirk walked slowly away from the white stone-and-
stucco house, along the rough road that served as a drive-
way. But here on Orand, there were no motor vehicles
to use the gravel and dirt paths, only carts drawn by the
native oxen and horses.

Orand and its people were stepchildren of nature. Or-
biting a backwater star, the planet hid no treasures beneath its parched surface. Possessed of neither wealth nor
strategic location, it held little interest for galactic profit-
eers and prospectors. But its sparse population of perhaps five million persevered, wringing a subsistence out
of an assortment of ventures—some farming, mining, a
little industry and trade.

In a way, Kirk felt sorry for the Orandi natives, with
their world doomed to be no more than a speck on a star
map. But its very forgettable nature is what made it the
perfect place for Stevvin's family to live out their exile.
For while Orand would never be rich and powerful, neither would it be a battlefield, as Shad had become. The
King would be safe here, able to fade into the drabness
that characterized this sad, sandy planet.

At first, the Klingons had kept a full surveillance team
on Orand; but when the war dragged on and on, the con-
tingent dwindled to a few agents, then finally to one
Klingon and a pair of paid Orandi informants who
watched the King's house and the comings and goings of
its occupants. The Klingons had come to believe that
Stevvin would never leave Orand, and their vigilance
slackened.

They were finally right, Kirk thought with bitterness
directed at himself. Had he done the King any good, convincing him to leave Shad? Or had he robbed a proud
ruler of his last chance to fight back? He couldn't have
known how things would turn out, but that didn't make
him feel any better. He wiped beads of sweat off his brow.
Orand was hot—that was what the name meant. *Hot as*

*hell,* loosely translated. The sun was dipping below the horizon, and a tentative breeze teased the scrub trees squatting on the dunes; but it was still stifling and Kirk retreated to the sanctuary of the house.

Centuries of the sun's ferocity had trained Orandi architects well. This house was over a hundred years old, but looked the same as buildings constructed yesterday—white exteriors, small windows high up on the walls, polished slate floors sunk several feet below outside ground level, and perpetually running fountains and pools in every room.

McCoy perched on the stone rim of the fountain in the library and rippled the pool's surface with his finger. He wondered if the builders had been psychologists, as well —the sound and feel of the trickling water made the place seem ten degrees cooler than it really was.

Spock sat in a soft chair, flipping through a Shaddan history book. They heard the tired clicking of boot heels, and Kirk entered from the hallway.

"Feel any better?" asked McCoy.

Kirk flexed his shoulders. "Nope. Just hot—and tired. Go for a hike, and the thin atmosphere really gets to you."

"You should feel at home, Spock," McCoy said. "This place is just as uncomfortable as Vulcan."

"I find it quite acceptable," Spock said mildly.

"You would." McCoy steered Kirk over to the fountain and sat him on the edge. "Dip your hand in there. You'll feel cooler in a minute."

"Is that a sound medical prescription?"

"Tested by the doctor himself."

Kirk followed instructions, and sprinkled a few drops of the icy water on his face—McCoy was right. He shook his head to clear it and took the chilled glass of punch McCoy handed to him. "How is he, Bones?"

"He's old, Jim. He just isn't up to taking an extended space voyage. I don't know if he'll die today, or next week. If he stayed here and rested, maybe he could hang on for months. But I don't think he'd make it to Shad. and even if, by some miracle, he *was* alive, he'd be in no condition to make stirring speeches or lead the big battle."

"Isn't there anything you can do?"

McCoy shook his head helplessly. "I can't reverse old age."

Kirk leaned forward, resting elbows on knees and head in hands. "Hell of a place to spend eighteen years."

"It could've been worse," McCoy offered. "Better than dying on Shad."

"Was it?" Kirk didn't bother to look up.

"Of course it was, Jim. They had some hope while they were here. And look, the King's lived long enough to know that things are looking up."

"But the idea, Doctor," Spock said, "was for the King to return, stabilize the geopolitical situation, and overcome devisive forces. Your medical report, which I am certain is accurate as usual, has effectively negated our mission."

McCoy glared. "You're so damned cold-blooded. That's a man we're talking about, a great man—and Jim's friend. Instead of—"

"Spock's right," Kirk said, raising a hand to cut him off. He took a deep breath. "And I don't know what to do about it."

"We're going to save Shad—*that's* what we're going to do about it, James."

The King's voice was hoarse and shaky—but his determination was firm. He sat up in bed, supported by several threadbare pillows; his body, wasted by age, looked like a child's under the quilt.

"But you can't go back," Kirk said gently.

Stevvin waved his hand—feeble yet clearly impatient. "I know all that. Dr. McCoy explained it all, even though I already knew it. Y'know, I haven't seen the outside of this house in two months. The servants offer to carry me out, but if I can't go under my own power . . ." His voice trailed off and his eyes closed.

Kirk flashed a concerned look at McCoy—and the King opened one wrinkled lid in time to see it.

"Just resting, James. Not gone yet."

"Why didn't you tell Star Fleet how you felt? Why did you say you were ready to go back?"

"Because I *am* ready. You'll all be old, someday, and you'll know that just because you *can't* do something doesn't mean you won't want to try to do it." He rested a moment again. "What would they have done if I told

them I was past the rabblerouser stage? Do you think
they'd have sent a starship just to be a king's hearse?"

Stevvin shifted weakly, then frowned in discomfort.
"Beds are for sleeping, not living in. The answer is, they
wouldn't have sent a *scout* ship. Even my servants don't
know how soon they may lose this master." Once more,
the old King paused.

"Your Highness, I'm glad we got to see each other
again. I never thought we would . . . but this mission of
unification isn't possible without your return."

"Not my return, James . . . the *monarch's* return. My
health—as well as the plan I'm about to tell you—must
be kept secret, even from Star Fleet. Only the four of us,
and my daughter Kailyn, will know. . . . You will return
*her* to Shad—to rule in my place."

McCoy paced near the library fountain. "Jim, how can
you completely change our mission without telling Star
Fleet? They'll court-martial you so fast, you won't have
time to change for the trial. It just isn't—"

"All right, Bones, all right. You made your point. What
about you, Spock? Would you care to add to the list of
obstacles?"

The first officer arched an eyebrow and stood for a
moment with his hands clasped behind him. "I disagree
with Dr. McCoy—"

"What else is new?" said McCoy.

"—but not entirely. I agree that you theoretically risk
harsh disciplinary action, altering specific Star Fleet orders on such an important mission. However, in practice,
charges are not often proffered when the mission suc-
ceeds."

McCoy stared. "A Vulcan counseling disobeying of orders?"

"The captain would not be disobeying. Our circumstances have changed—markedly—since those orders
were issued. The captain must make a command decision; if he follows the newly proposed course of action,
what is the probability of success?"

"Okay," said McCoy, "what *is* the probability of success?"

"I have not been asked to calculate it, Doctor. But I do
believe the odds in our favor will be reduced considerably
if we take the time to confer with Star Fleet and wait for

the bureaucracy to deliver its answer. We must act swiftly."

Kirk listened thoughtfully. "Is that your recommendation, Spock?"

"Tentatively. But before any final decision can be rendered, we must hear the King's plan in full detail, and ascertain his daughter's readiness to take her father's place."


The Crown Princess of Shad was tending her garden when Kirk found her.

"It's very impressive," he said, cupping a new blossom in his hands as he knelt on the path between rows of bushes, vines, and vegetables. "I didn't think a *cactus* could grow on this planet."

"It's not that hard," Kailyn said, averting her eyes as she spoke. Kirk noticed that she found it easier to look at a plant or a patch of dirt as they talked. When he caught her eye, she stammered ever so slightly.

"You built this whole irrigation system yourself?"

"No. I just designed it. The servants helped me pipe the water from the house and actually make it."

"How old were you then?"

"Twelve, Captain."

The last word—*captain*—caught his ear like a bramble. "Captain? Why so formal? What happened to 'Uncle Jim'?"

She bowed her head. "It's been so long. I . . . I never thought we'd see you again."

He touched her chin and gently lifted her face. She had the deep, dark eyes of her father. "I thought of you a lot," she said. "When Father and I would have our lessons, we'd stop and wonder where you were. We knew you'd become captain of the *Enterprise*." She looked away again. "I'd dream about you coming to take us home again."

"Did you mind being here, Kailyn?"

They walked on through the garden. "It's all I really know. I was only five when we left Shad." Her eyes roamed over the greenery and rainbow of petals, seeking plants that might need extra attention. To Kirk, it was all a mass of leaves; to Kailyn, no detail, no drooping branch or encroaching weed, was too small to spot and tend to.

Kailyn was twenty-three now, but she was small and

delicate, her manner tentative and cautious, like a lost fawn. Her eyes were wide and dark brown, almost black. And they were always moving; not nervously, but more as if they possessed an overwhelming curiosity all their own. Kailyn herself seemed timid, but the eyes peered piercingly at all they could touch, searching, learning all they could. Most of all, they were sad, even when she wasn't.

"What did your father teach you?"

"All about Shad—our history, how our family had ruled through times of feast and shortage, the Covenant with our people and our gods. How . . . how the Dynasty has to continue . . ."

"Through you."

"I know."

"Then you know what your father has planned?"

"Yes." She reached down and slipped her hand into Kirk's as they sat on a rough wooden bench. He noticed the first stars were twinkling in the midnight-blue twilight sky. "Oh, Uncle Jim, I love my father. I . . . I guess I worship him. He's protected me all these years, been both mother and father, given me his dream." She took a breath, then spoke in a small, halting voice. "But I don't think I can do it. I don't have his strength."

"How do you know?"

"I feel it in him when he talks to me, even weak as he is now. I know he's dying, but when he calls me in and we talk about what it'll be like to be home again, he makes me believe. His strength makes me see what he sees. But . . . but when I leave him and come out here to watch the stars, I can't feel it anymore. What will it be like when he's gone, when I won't be able to go in there and have him lift me up again?"

"I don't know, Kailyn."

This time, she did look into Kirk's eyes, and there was a steadfastness in hers that made him want to say, *You do have it . . . if only you could see into yourself . . . the strength is there.* But she would have to discover that for herself.

"He taught me history, my place in our religion, told me the feelings I should have. I don't know why, but it wasn't enough."

"Are you . . . afraid of being Queen?"

"Yes." It was a fast answer, almost a relief. Then her

voice dropped to a whisper. "More than that . . . how does someone learn to be a savior?"

"Those doubts aren't the only thing," McCoy said as he sat with Captain Kirk and Spock in the library. There's another root to the problem, Jim. Kailyn has an incurable disease."

"*What?* What is it?"

"Choriocytosis."

"But that almost killed Spock in a matter of days when he had it. If we hadn't tracked down the Orion pirates and gotten that drug back—"

"My case was acute," Spock said. "I believe Kailyn's is chronic."

"That's right. His case was caused by a virus, Jim. Kailyn's is an inborn hormone deficiency. It's pretty rare, but it's treatable with daily injections. In addition, the disease affects different races in different ways."

Kirk recalled what he knew about choriocytosis from Spock's almost fatal bout with it several years earlier, how the virus encased his copper-based blood cells, preventing them from carrying the oxygen needed for life functions. McCoy explained the variations between acute and chronic forms. Kailyn had inherited a recessive genetic condition that inhibited production of the hormone holulin—a substance present in the bodies of about a dozen humanoid species, though not Earth humans. Injections made up for the lack of holulin, keeping blood cells free of the suffocating shell-like membrane formed by choriocytosis.

"As long as she takes the shots," McCoy said, "she should live a fairly normal life, though some complications may set in during old age. It's a little like diabetes was to humans before it was cured."

"If it went untreated, would it affect her the same as it did Spock?"

"Yes. First unconsciousness, then coma, then death."

"There's a 'but' in your voice, Bones."

"It gets worse under stress, and she's going to be in for a lot of that, Jim. Holulin production can stop altogether and careful treatment is absolutely necessary."

"Is Kailyn fully aware of her condition and all that it entails, Doctor?" asked Spock.

"Oh, she's aware—but she thinks of herself as crippled

because of it. She told me she's afraid to give herself the injections. One of the servants does it. Chronic choriocytosis can be a big psychological barrier, and that's what it is to her. If she can't handle her own illness, Jim, how can she guide the destiny of a whole planet?"

Kirk had no answer. Kailyn had one—deep within herself. But would she ever find it?

# Chapter Four

*. . . And it came to pass that the second god Dal saw the long table Keulane made; and Dal said: "Was this made from one piece, whole, cut in a single stroke from the heart of the largest tree in the land?"*

*Unbowed (for he feared not the god Dal), Keulane spake: "Yes, and with my own hand. Let this table replace the field of battle. Let the people reveal their hearts with true words and not sword thrusts. Let this wood, from the tree's heart, be the heart of Shad, one world united forever."*

*And Dal answered: "It shall be, Keulane. I shall give you dominion over Things and Creatures-Not-Man."*

*And the god Dal gave his blessing, rendering the sword of Keulane, that cut the tree in a single stroke, as Strength with dominion over Things and Creatures-Not-Man. Keulane added this to his dominions over Heaven, given by the fourth god Koh; and over Land and Sea, given by the third god Adar. It remained for him to gain the blessing of the first god Iyan, God among Gods, and dominion over Man.*

*And so Keulane waited, for he felt it was his reward, but Iyan came not to him. At long last, Keulane cried out: "Have I not earned this?"*

*A bolt of blinding light and roaring thunder smote the sword from Keulane's hands, and he trembled at the voice of Iyan, God of Gods: "You are foolish, Keulane. No man can have dominion over Men. You*

*can only guide them. We will not speak to you again
in this life. We will never speak directly unto you
again, but we will give you this."*

*And the hand of Iyan placed the Crown of Shad
upon Keulane's head. It was of silver, and of crystals, a pair whose inner depths were murky and
fogged to the eye and mind of man. "Do you hear
and see my voice?"*

*Keulane answered that he did, but he did not, for
the eyes and ears of his heart were closed by fear.
Iyan knew, and he shook Keulane to his very soul.
"Hear me!"*

*And lo, the crystals of the Crown became clear
through, with the blue of Heaven as their shade. And
Keulane felt his heart open, and he saw clearly, and
heard. He knew the echoes of the past, and felt the
tides of Time. And he knew the roads the People of
Shad would take, if only he could lead them there.*

*"You have the Power of Times," Iyan told him.
"Thus shall you and your sons and daughters lead.
Of the children you beget, only special ones in their
time will have the Power. They will wear the Crown,
the crystals will give them sight, and the People will
hail them as Kings and Queens of the Covenant. . . .*

—Book of Shad,
Verse of Keulane

"I read it," McCoy said, replacing the book on the library shelf. "But I'm not sure I believe it. It sounds like
something out of the legends of King Arthur."

"On the contrary, it is more reminiscent of stories from
your Earth bible," Spock said. "Or Vulcan lore about
Surak and the founding of our modern philosophy and
way of life. Almost all religions and cultural heritages
share that common factor—a tendency to mythologize
those elements that gave rise to them in the first place,
blending probable facts with a modicum of the superna-
tural or inexplicable."

"You're right, now that I recall those Biblical stories,"
Kirk said.

"Does that mean you believe those tales about the
Crown, and the crystals changing color?" McCoy asked.

Before Kirk could answer, Spock jumped back in. "It
is no less credible than Moses and the parting of the Red

Sea, or Jesus feeding the multitudes, or Surak turning back the Army of Ten Thousand."

McCoy shook his head. "But all those stories have been explained in some scientific, rational way."

"So has the Crown of Shad. Before King Stevvin was forced to flee, some scientific research was done. The Power of Times is known to be an ESP-like phenomenon involving brain waves of a particular frequency and intensity. A person with the Power produces just the right brain waves to clear the electromagnetically sensitive crystals. This has been duplicated via computer simulation."

McCoy remained unconvinced, and Kirk half-smiled as the doctor parried. "But that still doesn't explain the other part, the mystical hearing of the gods' voices, that sixth sense of a fortune-teller."

"If you had carefully read the Book of Shad, Doctor, you would know that the Power does not open the mind to a literal foretelling of future events. It merely permits a sensing of the flow of people and things, somewhat more accurately than a mere educated guess. But I hardly expect you, as a nontelepathic creature, to fully grasp the concept," Spock concluded.

Kirk decided the discussion had gone on long enough. "It's not important whether we believe in the Shaddan religion, but the people of Shad take it very seriously. The monarch of the Covenant is more than just a political leader. Whoever sits on that throne is also their religious leader, and they won't accept someone who doesn't wear the Crown as proof of the Power of Times."

It was that simple—the mysterious Crown had been on the head of every Shaddan ruler since Keulane, and no one could rule without it. But a pair of exceedingly large problems loomed in King Stevvin's plan, and Kirk wasn't sure which of the two might be worse.

First, the King did not have the Crown. Because of its sacred significance, it was imperative that it never fall into the hands of the Mohd Alliance or the Klingon Empire. Thus, when he left Shad in the confusion of civil war, Stevvin had spirited the Crown away with him and hid it on a planet almost as far off the beaten track as Orand, in a location known to no one but himself. The spot was to be revealed to his successor only; had he or Kailyn died before returning to Shad, he would have taken the secret to his grave, ending the Dynasty forever.

In order for Kailyn to be accepted as lawful Queen, the Crown had to be found and taken safely back to Shad along with the King's daughter. This presented a complex problem of logistics—admittedly dangerous and shot through with chances for disaster, but one over which Kirk could still exert a fair amount of influence, if not outright control.

The second puzzle, however, had no tangible pieces for him to lay his hands upon. In fact, the only answers were within Kailyn. Did this young woman—more child than adult—possess the stuff of leadership, the will to complete what her father had set in motion? And most important of all, *did she have the Power of Times?*

That they didn't know, and wouldn't, until and unless the Crown could be retrieved and placed upon her head, a head filled with self-doubt. Doubt that could overwhelm the Power even if she did have it.

She was the last of her generation, the final scion of the royal family. And if she failed, that was it—no Power, no monarchy, no restoration of unity, no victory on Shad, no mission. On the frail shoulders of a frightened girl rested the future of her planet and all of Quadrant J-221.

# Chapter Five

*Captain's Log:* Star Date 7816.1

We have completed step one of King Stevvin's plan
—the King, his daughter, and their four servants
have left Orand on board the *Enterprise*, as expected by both Star Fleet Command and any
Klingon agents who may have been watching. His
royal highness has lived long enough to serve as an
all-important decoy. The Klingons know the Crown
must be retrieved, and they expect us to lead them
to its hiding place—but we'll do no such thing. While
the *Enterprise* instead leads them on a circuitous
wild goose chase, Mr. Spock and Dr. McCoy will
take a specially outfitted shuttlecraft and accompany the King's daughter to Sigma 1212, the icy
world where Stevvin hid his sacred Crown eighteen
years ago. If all goes well, the shuttle crew will retrieve the Crown, rendezvous with the *Enterprise*,
and allow us to complete our mission of reunification.
I hope King Stevvin can somehow live long enough
to see his plan come to a successful end.

There was no royal suite aboard the *Enterprise*, and if
McCoy had his way, the King would have been in sick
bay proper. But Kirk managed to effect a compromise—
a diagnostic bed was set up in VIP quarters, giving the
King privacy and comfort, and McCoy the constant mon-
itoring of medical data he demanded. The surgeon knew

the odds against Stevvin's making it all the way to Shad, but he was going to try his damnedest to beat them.

The King was reading when Kirk entered the cabin, and he smiled as the captain sat by the bedside. Kirk glanced at the computer screen.

*"Don Quixote?"*

"One of the best presents you ever gave me, James. I read that book so many times over these last years. I'd like to have met Cervantes. Any man who could have created such a dreamer as Quixote must have been very special."

"It's always been one of my favorites, too," Kirk agreed. Then he turned pensive. "I wonder if I would've had the courage he had, to hold on to those dreams when everything and everybody tried to snuff them out."

Stevvin laid a gnarled hand on Kirk's arm. "You have that courage."

"You're so sure of things . . ."

The old man chuckled wryly and his eyes sparkled. "I look back on all the times I should have been sure, and wasn't. And now I don't have time for doubts. Maybe that was the source of Don Quixote's strength—maybe the young can't tilt at windmills because they have too much life to lose . . . the old man has no place to go but the next life. Why not die a little sooner than a little later?"

Kirk's brow furrowed. "The closer death comes, the less you fear it?"

"So it seems. When I was your age, I never would've believed it. But when you give up little bits of yourself— eyesight goes, voice becomes hoarse, breathing's a chore you'd consider avoiding, legs can't take more than four steps without a rest, arms can't carry a child anymore, even the mind begins to wander back to how it used to be —before you know it, there isn't much left to give up. And then the fear goes, too—if you're lucky." He paused for a shallow breath, and Kirk could hear the lung-deep wheeze. "I've been lucky, James."

The King's eyes slipped shut, and Kirk stood to leave. But Stevvin's hand held him with a firm grip; Kirk smiled at that sign of life not yet surrendered.

"Stay," whispered Stevvin, and Kirk sat again. "Things are going well so far?"

"So far."

The old King caught the hint of concern in Kirk's voice. "You're still uncertain about Kailyn."

Kirk wanted to say something reassuring, but that wasn't how he truly felt, and he couldn't lie to the King.

"Even if the Crown proves she has the Power of Times, that's no guarantee she can rule the planet. Not all children can do what their parents wish of them."

"True, it's no certainty. In the end, it's still the strength and qualities of the person on the throne. But don't underestimate the Power and what it means. I know it sounds to an outsider like black magic, but it does exist, and it does help one who possesses it transcend the human frailties we're all born with. To use it, James, one must have absolute faith. Mine faltered—perhaps I caused my own downfall." He shrugged his thin shoulders under the metallic sheen of the blanket. "But my belief was rekindled when I knew you were coming to take us back. I sensed that the life currents that carried us apart were bringing us back together. It took me this long to comprehend that faith springs not just from gods—or from your one god—but from fellowmen as well. We must rely upon others—and be worthy of reliance ourselves. Kailyn will have to learn this if she's to lead. I think she will."

In the silence, Kirk wondered—was it wisdom, or foolish faith? The intercom whistled and Kirk touched the button; McCoy's frown filled the small screen.

"Jim, you're tiring out my patient. Your Highness, just because he's the captain, don't feel you can't toss him out if you'd rather rest."

"On the contrary, Doctor, his visit has been refreshing. Like the chats we used to have back home."

"Well, okay for now. But my prescription says you need some sleep, your Highness. Vamoose, Jim."

"Dr. McCoy," said Stevvin, "is there any room in that prescription for a spot of brandy?"

McCoy lifted an eyebrow, and scratched his chin. "Jim, how do you say no to a royal patient?"

"You don't. You just bring the brandy to the royal cabin and fill a royal glass."

"Just this once," McCoy said. "And right after, we'll both leave said royal patient to get some shut-eye. Agreed, Captain?"

"Yes, sir," Kirk said, saluting the viewscreen. The page

of *Don Quixote* grew bold again over McCoy's fading image.

"Do you think we could get him to agree to a tour of the ship?" asked Stevvin, with real anticipation in his tone.

"I think that might be pressing our luck. But we'll give it a try."

Much to Kirk's surprise, his medical officer gave in on the tour idea, so long as he came along. Kailyn accompanied them as well, and they pushed Stevvin along in a wheelchair. There were no wheels, of course; the orthopedic support couch glided atop an anti-grav field, making the heaviest patient easy to maneuver. The King beamed with fatherly pride as Kirk played sightseeing guide at each stop.

And Kailyn truly felt like a tourist. She was awed by the vastness of the *Enterprise*, and by Captain Kirk's sure grasp of every detail of every operation.

"It only *seems* like he knows everything," McCoy whispered, loudly enough for Kirk to overhear.

"Right," Kirk nodded. "Actually, Dr. McCoy knows everything."

The group laughed and moved on—nearly running head-on into Sulu and Chekov jogging around a corridor junction.

"Whoa, gentlemen! There's a place for this, and it's not all over the ship."

Sulu breathed lightly as he answered with a sheepish smile. "Sorry, sir. But Chekov just wasn't getting into the spirit of running on the treadmill track. I think he needs to feel the breeze through his hair, watch the scenery pass by . . ."

McCoy regarded the wheezing security chief, doubled over and collapsed against the wall. "Personally, I think he needs a stretcher."

"Oh, he's just getting warmed up," said Sulu. He nudged Chekov on the shoulder, almost knocking him over. "Another mile or so, and then back to the gym for a little fencing. Come on, Chekov. Rest too long and you'll get cramps. See you all later." Sulu leaped ahead and disappeared around the corner.

Chekov leaned away from the sympathetic wall, swaying for a moment. "With friends like this, who needs Klingons?"

He staggered away and Kirk resumed the tour.

So many resources at his disposal, Kailyn thought. So many people and skills at his fingertips. She'd never been on anything like this starship, except a planet, a world. That's what the *Enterprise* was, in reality—a self-contained world, and Kirk was its king.

*He surveys it with such confidence, such pleasure,* she marveled. He was sovereign ruler here, as Kailyn would have to be. As her ailing father had been years ago. She wondered if he had taken to command as comfortably as Kirk seemed to. Would the mantle of responsibility and power ever fit so well on her?

King Stevvin fell asleep shortly after returning to his quarters; McCoy paused a moment to check the monitors, and he didn't like what they told him. The strain of the tour probably hadn't made any difference, but the King of Shad was slipping slowly closer to death. The doctor kept it to himself as Kirk headed up to the bridge, and Kailyn went to her own cabin, adjacent to her father's, to rest.

McCoy stalked into his office and watched the door slide shut, cutting him off from the corridor with a perfunctory hiss. "Dammit," he grumbled. "No doors to slam on this ship." And so he pounded his fist on the nearest countertop instead; but it wasn't the same and he longed for an old-fashioned slammable door and the room-shaking crash it would make.

His annoyance stemmed from two sources—the first, his inability to do anything about the King's inevitable demise. The second . . . the second made his blood run cold. He'd looked at Stevvin in the wheelchair—and he'd seen himself, an old man, helpless as a babe . . . being fed, or trundled from place to place. He looked in the mirror again, at the wrinkles collected by years of too many late hours in too many labs, regrets lingering from his ill-fated marriage, worries about his daughter Joanna, now grown and practically a stranger to him, the taste of a few extra drinks he could've passed up.

*Water under the bridge,* he thought with a mental shrug. *Even Vulcans get wrinkles. Besides, facial creases don't mean I'm old. It's what you think you are—and right now, I think I'm old. Hell, what would I do if a woman came in here right now and—*

The question was interrupted by the office door sliding open. Kailyn entered and looked about like a nervous sparrow.

"Dr. McCoy," she blurted, "I want to learn how to give myself the holulin injections."

McCoy frowned. "Not now, Kailyn," he said, more gruffly than he'd intended. "I've got some things I—"

Before he could complete the thought, she was gone, as quietly and unexpectedly as she'd come, and he found himself staring at the closing door.

*Dammit. Why the hell did I do that?* He shook his head ruefully. *So a woman walks in and I send her right back out again. Wait a minute—she's just a girl, and the King's daughter to boot. And that doesn't count.*

He rolled his eyes. *Of course it counts. She came for help, and you're too busy feeling sorry for yourself.*

"Sometimes you're an incredible jackass, McCoy," he said out loud, and quickly went out to find Kailyn.

It took some effort, but with a combination of Southern charm and fatherly coaxing, McCoy managed to convince Kailyn to come back to the office. He was surprised at how little she knew of her own serious illness, and he determined that self-injection would have to wait until he could give her as comprehensive a medical education as possible before they left the *Enterprise* to search for the Crown.

But if her specific knowledge of choriocytosis was limited, her ability to absorb and understand physiological facts and their interrelationships was nothing short of remarkable. McCoy figured she must have had the equivalent of a university master's degree, taught entirely by the King during the long wait on Orand, and his admiration of both father and daughter grew. As the complexity of their lessons increased, so did Kailyn's enthusiasm.

McCoy was preparing the next study tape when Kailyn arrived early for their session. She took a seat while he transferred several diagrams from the computer file on choriocytosis, and she listened closely to the music cassette playing in the background. The piece had a subtle Latin rhythm, intricate instrumental harmonies alternating with a lusty flourish of brass.

"Melendez," Kailyn said after a few minutes.

McCoy looked up from his computer terminal. "Hmm?"

"Melendez. Carlos Juan Melendez . . . the composer."

McCoy laughed. "How do you know an early-twenty-first-century Earth musician from Texas?"

"I love music. I was one of those children who took lessons and couldn't get enough to keep me happy. I wanted to learn every instrument we had—and a few we didn't."

"I'm beginning to think there's nothing you can't do."

Kailyn closed her eyes and sighed. "I still can't give myself the injections."

"Don't worry. It's just a mental block," he said, putting an arm around her. "Everybody's got their little quirks. To this day, I still can't swallow a pill without something to wash it down—like brandy."

She smiled a not very convincing smile and leaned her head on his shoulder. He inhaled the garden-fresh fragrance of her hair, and felt a little less elderly for the first time since the birthday party.

"Where's Dr. McCoy?" asked Kirk.

Christine Chapel's preoccupation with a lab work-up on the King was momentarily disrupted. "With his shadow," she said absently.

"His what?"

"I mean, I think he went with Kailyn to visit her father, Captain."

Kirk nodded. "By the way, I did hear you the first time. Exactly what did that mean?"

"Nothing, sir."

"Ahh. It just sort of . . . slipped out."

"Something like that, sir."

Kirk bounced on his heels for a moment, gazing expectantly at Chapel. Clearly, she was torn between saying what she really had on her mind or crawling into the nearest test tube in the hopes that Captain Kirk would go away and forget her slip. But he stayed, and finally she couldn't stand the silence.

"I'm not trying to gossip, Captain, but she always seems to be around him. He goes to the labs, she's with him. To the ship's mess, she's at his table. The only times she's not around him are when she's with her father."

"It doesn't seem to be any cause for alarm, does it?"

"I guess not, sir."

"Besides, McCoy's a good father figure, isn't he?"

"I wouldn't know, Captain," Chapel said with a slight blush coming to her cheeks. "And I'm not so sure she thinks of him in a completely fatherly way."

Kirk suppressed a smile. "Well, maybe it'll make him feel a little more youthful, having a young lady pay attention to him."

"As long as he doesn't get carried away."

"Are you afraid he's not aware of what's happening? He *is* a pretty fair psychologist."

"Captain, you know as well as I do that physicians don't always heal themselves."

"Touché, Doctor. I'll mention it to McCoy—when I can find him without the young lady."

"Discreetly please, sir," she implored.

"I'll do my best."

"Christine put you up to this, didn't she, Jim?"

"That's ridiculous, Bones," Kirk said quickly.

"Not if I know Chapel," McCoy countered, sitting on his bunk and pulling his boots off with one grunt per foot. He rubbed his toes to restore circulation. "They should get a new podiatric specialist to design some decent boots for Star Fleet."

"I'm not here to discuss your feet."

"No, you're here to discuss my private life," McCoy snapped.

"Calm down. Your private life isn't the problem."

"There *isn't* any problem!"

"But there *could* be if you get involved with Kailyn in any way."

McCoy stood up abruptly, began pacing, and abandoned all efforts at hiding his annoyance. "So we eat a couple of meals together, listen to some music, go over the implications of her illness . . . is that so terrible? Look, Jim, I want that girl to be able to administer her own shots by the time we leave this ship. To do it, I've got to get her to trust me. If that means being nice to her and getting to know her, well, *dammit*, that's what I'll do."

"And *is* that what you're doing?"

"Yes!" said McCoy, waving his arms. "Good lord, if I questioned everything *you* did that I thought was a little screwy, neither of us would ever get a stitch of work done."

Kirk eyed his ship's surgeon, then pursed his lips. "Now, *that's* the diplomatic Leonard McCoy explanation I was waiting to hear."

McCoy shook his head. "Get out of here and let me get my beauty sleep. Lord knows, at my age I need it."

Kirk's own rest period was the type to add wrinkles and subtract years—most of it spent tossing and turning, willing his eyes to stay closed, then opening them the moment his mind wandered from the task of sleeping to the vagaries of their mission. Any further thoughts of slumber were destroyed by the whistle of the intercom.

"Bridge to Captain Kirk," said Sulu.

Kirk leaned over and touched the switch. "Kirk here, Mr. Sulu. What's up—other than me?"

"Sorry to disturb you, sir, but we thought you'd want to know we're being followed by a Klingon cruiser."

Kirk rolled to his feet and grabbed his shirt off the bed in a single move. "On my way."

The bridge was calm and quiet as Kirk stepped out of the turbolift. "Report," he said, looking first to Sulu, who commanded this watch.

"No hostile action on their part, sir. They're just hovering out there, almost out of sensor range. We tried some leisurely evasive maneuvers. They're not exactly following us to the letter, but every time we'd lose them, they'd turn up again in a minute or two."

"Any communications, Uhura?"

"Nothing, Captain. I hailed them on all frequencies . . . no response."

"I guess they had nothing to say," Kirk said as he eased into the command seat.

"Shall I try them again, sir?"

"No. We know they're there. That's all we need to know right now. Chekov, keep an eye on them. I wouldn't want to lose them."

Kirk sat back. *So, they've taken the bait . . . doing exactly what we hoped they'd do. But it's just too easy. We'll have to stay sharp—Klingons are rarely so cooperative.*

# Chapter Six

McCoy and Kailyn stood side by side, gazing out the recreation deck's huge observation port. From their perch near the stern of the main saucer section, they could see the Engineering hull below and the *Enterprise*'s slender engine nacelles fanning out gracefully, bathed in the gentle glow of the ship's own floodlights.

Kailyn seemed determined to find out everything about McCoy's past, where he'd been, what he'd done, whom he'd known, how he'd come to be a physician with Star Fleet. And he enjoyed answering the questions.

Eventually, she wrapped one arm around his waist, and he noticed that she was leaning on him for support. She was pale.

"What's wrong?"

"My stomach's a little queasy," she said with a lop-sided, little-girl smile. "This is the first time I realized we're out in the middle of space on a tiny little ship."

"I'd hardly call the *Enterprise* tiny."

Kailyn leaned forward, pressing up against the port window. The ship was moving, of course, but she had the strangest sensation that they were suspended among the stars, just another heavenly body. The stars . . . so many of them, wherever she might look, set like unblinking jewels strewn across the infinite darkness. So many of them—yet, they seemed uncrowded, unhurried as they moved ever farther from the center of the Universe on a journey that had commenced with the beginning of all things, the beginning of time.

She drifted out of her reverie, back to McCoy, who watched with a mixture of fascination and concern.

"What were you thinking about, Kailyn?"

She shrugged. "I don't know. A lot of things. There's so much out there. When we went to Orand, I was so young, I didn't even realize what was happening."

"You mean being out in space?"

She nodded.

McCoy chuckled. "Everybody's like this on their first space voyage. You think you know what it'll be like—until you're actually on that ship and get out in the middle of nowhere. I've had more space rookies stumble into my office—all of a sudden, reality hits them, and they get this *look* on their faces . . ."

He pressed his nose to hers and his eyes bugged out, like a surprised insect. Kailyn couldn't help laughing, and he stepped back, his hands on her shoulders.

"Now, *that's* more like it. You're too young not to laugh more."

But her smile suddenly faded and she lowered her eyes. McCoy touched her cheek. "What is it?"

She didn't look up. "Am I too young?"

"For what?"

"For everything. To be Queen of Shad . . . to give my own shots . . ." There was a long pause. "To love someone."

Now it was McCoy's turn for a lingering moment of silence. To love someone—did she mean him? *Poppycock. Now I'm thinking like Christine.* Before he could formulate a response, the intercom whistled urgently.

"Dr. McCoy," said Uhura's voice. "Report to sick bay immediately. Dr. McCoy, to sick bay, please." Her tone said *emergency* without using the word, and McCoy reflexively grabbed Kailyn's hand and pulled her toward the turbolift.

The captain and Spock stood outside the doctor's office ready to intercept him. When Kirk saw Kailyn with McCoy, his jaw tightened for just a second; there was no way to protect her.

"Bones, it's the King." Then he turned and led the way down the corridor to Stevvin's quarters.

Kailyn held fast to McCoy's hand, her mind racing from thought to thought, careening between fear, resignation, and a determination to keep her wits about her. Tears formed in her eyes, but stayed there.

Dr. Chapel and a medical aide were already at the King's bedside, administering an injection and oxygen. They stepped smoothly aside when McCoy entered, and Chapel delivered a succinct report. Kailyn watched and listened dully, absorbing blurred impressions, clearly hearing only two words: *"Heart failure."*

Kirk guided Kailyn back toward a corner of the room, and they stood with Spock as the medical team worked with no wasted motions or words. The life-function indicators above the bed jumped and sagged erratically. Chapel placed a portable heart-lung machine over the King's chest, while the med tech adjusted the oxygen feed. McCoy punched several control buttons when Chapel nodded to him, and the cardio-stimulator began a steady pulse, its green light blinking evenly.

"Pulse and pressure stabilized, Doctor," Chapel said finally.

"Breathing on his own," the med tech added.

McCoy stepped back and wiped his forehead. "Leave the cardio-stimulator in place for now, Doctor. Keep an eye on the readouts."

Chapel nodded and she and the young aide exited. For the first time, McCoy looked at Kailyn. She broke away from Kirk and buried her face on McCoy's shoulder. He nodded to Kirk and Spock and they left McCoy and Kailyn alone. For a long time, he held her, and the only sounds were her sniffling and the faint beating of the cardio-stimulator.

Kailyn's eyes were red-rimmed, but she was all business for the strategy session with McCoy, Spock and Captain Kirk in the main briefing room. The details of the mission were raked over one more time. Kirk wanted to be certain not only that she knew the location of the Crown on Sigma 1212, but that she was psychologically ready for the task. After an hour, he sent her back to her cabin to rest.

"Opinions, gentlemen?" he asked, when she had gone.

"I think she's ready," McCoy said. "She seems to have gained a lot of self-confidence over these last three days, Jim. I was especially pleased by the way she bounced back from that crisis with her father this afternoon."

"I must differ, Captain," Spock said.

"Spock," snapped McCoy, "this is no time for nit-picking."

Spock ignored McCoy and addressed Kirk directly. "The young lady was disturbed to a great degree during the medical emergency. She seems unready to accept that her father will not live much longer, and I am forced to point out that this does not bode well for her ability to function without his support."

McCoy jumped to his feet. "Jim, she was upset," he argued. "That's normal—for a *human*, Mr. Spock. You both saw her here. She was clearheaded and alert, and I think that's pretty admirable under the circumstances." He sat back again. "I think this afternoon, seeing that equipment used on her father, was the first time Kailyn really faced the fact that he's dying. Oh, she understood it intellectually before, but emotionally it just hit her all at once. She cried, but she bounced back."

McCoy glanced from Kirk to Spock several times, inviting riposte or agreement. Spock merely raised an eyebrow. "I have stated my concern—and I believe Dr. McCoy has adequately explained the situation."

"I agree," Kirk concluded. "Besides, we don't have much choice, and we have no time to waste. Star Fleet will be expecting a report, and I'd like to be able to tell them 'mission accomplished.' "

Spock rose from his seat. "With your permission, sir, I shall return to the bridge."

Kirk nodded, and when Spock had left, he turned to the still-seated McCoy. "I want to believe you, Bones, that she'll get through this. Are you sure?"

"I'd put money on it."

The next few hours were devoted to mental and physical preparation. Kirk repeatedly went over the plan in his mind. He wanted to know every weak spot, to anticipate every surprise, to expect every possible intrusion of the unexpected.

Spock inspected the shuttle *Galileo*, specially equipped for long-distance travel with light-speed boosters, extra fuel, food rations, medical supplies, and survival items. A computer check revealed all systems ready, and a manual review confirmed it.

McCoy gathered the medical gear he'd need to care for

Kailyn if her choriocytosis flared seriously. And he did plenty of thinking—about Kailyn, about himself, and what was happening between them. *She's a child, younger than my daughter—and she's got a crush on you, McCoy. So what? I couldn't be interested in her like that. I'm a teacher, someone for her to look up to. It could just as easily have been Spock, if she went for logical, unemotional types. Her father won't be with her much longer—she's just transferring her feelings from him to me. She'll understand that—she's got to.*

Still, she was intelligent, gentle, pretty. *Why couldn't I be interested in her? Just because I really am old enough to be her father? How do you* feel, *McCoy?* He gave a mental shrug. *That's the hell of it—I don't know.*


"I can't stay long, Father," Kailyn said. "I don't want to tire you out."

Stevvin smiled weakly. The machines had been removed, but he had to remain flat on his back. He reached out with a trembling hand and she held it, resting it on the bed.

"You'll be leaving soon. Remember—Shirn O'tay was the patriarch. He'll show you where the Crown—"

"I know, Father, I know. Don't worry."

"I won't. Actually, I *will*—but that's a father's privilege."

Stevvin pulled his daughter's hand to his lips and kissed it. "The gods will care for you. And you have some good men to help you."

The King's breath came in short, labored rasps, and Kailyn fought back her tears. "I love you, Father."

He smiled and pressed her hand to his lips again.


"Sensor report," said Kirk.

Chekov looked up from the viewer at the science station. "The Klingon cruiser is just out of range, sir. They couldn't detect the shuttle launch now."

"Shuttle engine ignition, Captain," said Sulu.

Kirk punched up the *Galileo*'s channel on his intercom panel. "Kirk to *Galileo*."

"Spock here, Captain. All systems ready for shuttle launch."

"Spock . . ." Kirk hesitated. "Good luck. Kailyn, take good care of my officers. Especially McCoy."

Her voice was strong. "I will."

"Request shuttle bay doors open," Spock said.

Sulu flipped a console switch. "Shuttle bay doors open."

Kirk glanced at the hangar deck on the screen over the science station. "Launch shuttle."

Sulu's fingers skipped across the panel, deftly touching the final toggle. "Shuttle away, sir."

That night, King Stevvin, the seventeenth monarch in the Dynasty of Shad, died in his sleep with Captain Kirk and four royal servants at his side.

The shuttlecraft *Galileo* was ten hours out on its journey by that time. The King's plan for bringing peace to his world once and for all was progressing without him, as he had hoped it would. Even the Klingon cruiser resumed its place, following the *Enterprise*. All was as it should have been.

Except for one thing. Unknown to Kirk, or to the crew of the *Galileo*, when the shuttle passed through the outer reaches of a nondescript white-dwarf star system, far out of sensor range of the *Enterprise*, a shadow joined the excursion.

The shadow was a Klingon spy scout, manned by four intelligence agents. Their assignment was simple—follow the shuttlecraft. If its crew retrieved the holy Crown of Shad, kill them and claim the Crown for the Klingon Empire. And if they failed to find the Crown, kill them anyway.

# Chapter Seven

"Klingons, Kirk," Harrington barked with uncharacteristic fury. "The bloody Klingons knew before I did. If their secret communications network weren't so leaky, they'd know, and I *still* wouldn't know. Would you care to offer an explanation as to why you disobeyed orders?"

Kirk sat hunched over his desk, with Scotty standing directly behind him. On the viewscreen, the admiral was still in his robe—he'd obviously been roused from a good night's sleep with the news that the Klingons were on to the *Enterprise* decoy plan—a decoy plan *he'd* known nothing about.

"I'm sorry, Admiral," Kirk began. Not quite certain of what else to say, he moved on cautiously. "The situation was not as we were led to expect when we arrived at Orand, sir. You're aware that the Crown of Shad was not with the King when we—"

"Yes, Kirk. The bloody Klingon report we got hold of was quite clear in that detail."

"Once we ascertained that we couldn't go back to Shad without it, we also realized that the King was simply not healthy enough to make the extra trip. None of this was included in the briefing report we were given at Star Base, sir."

Kirk shot a quick glance back at Scott, who understood his captain's strategy—shifting a bit of the blame for the altered mission onto Star Fleet Intelligence.

"All right, Captain, I accept that the mission required modification and I'll even accept that the time involved in consulting with H.Q. might have blown the whole affair.

You're an accomplished starship captain, and you sit in that command seat because Star Fleet trusts your judgment —though right now, I might be convinced to question that."

Kirk swallowed, but continued to look head-on at the viewscreen.

"We've got two major problems to contend with, Kirk. First and foremost, it appears that one of the Shaddans aboard your ship is a Klingon agent, and second—"

"Begging your pardon, sir, but our shuttle crew out there on Sigma is going to be at the wrong end of a Klingon shooting gallery the second they find that Crown—"

"I am aware of that, Captain."

*"That's* our primary concern, sir. It's of the utmost importance that we get back to Sigma as quickly as possible in case the shuttle party needs assistance."

"Negative, Captain," Harrington said sharply. "If you'd been here when we got word from Intelligence, you'd know that rooting out the turncoat in the King's party is top priority."

"But the safety of the King's daughter and my officers—"

"—is of deep concern. However, Star Fleet will not be made fools of. The Klingons did just that, Captain. Here they had a spy under our noses all this time, you pull a plan out of nowhere that the Fleet doesn't even know about—and the enemy knows where you're going and when before you even get under way. *I* have to answer to superiors, too, and they *will not stand for that.* They threw it at me and I'm throwing it right to you. This is an order—find that spy."

"Sir, for all practical purposes, we have all four suspects in custody. We can investigate *after* we've ensured the safety of the shuttle mission."

"The Joint Chiefs of Staff want that spy secured first."

"Did the Joint Chiefs have any good ideas how to do that?" said Kirk, biting off each word—sidestepping the urge to illuminate them with colorful adjectives and verbs.

"You got into this, Kirk, and it's up to you to think of a way out. That's not a direct quote, I might add. The language here was a bit more descriptive."

Kirk was immediately sorry he'd restrained himself; the phrases running through his mind were *quite* descriptive, but he realized that insubordination was not the thing to help his cause at the moment.

"Admiral, I must register a strong protest. We—"

"That's your right, Captain. And these are your orders —formulate a plan to catch that spy, and hold your present position until you've got one. Then submit the specifics for our approval *before* you put it into effect. Is that clear?"

"Yes, sir," Kirk said tightly.

"One other thing—how is the King through all this?"

Kirk and Scott traded quick glances. "The King? The King is fine, sir."

"Good. I'd hate to have any more complications after all this. Very well . . . we shall be expecting a plan from you in exactly two hours. Star Fleet out."

Harrington's image faded to black, and Kirk rested his chin on his arms, slumped over the desktop.

Scotty shook his head soberly. "Captain, y' lied to a Star Fleet admiral."

"Let's hope you and I are the only ones who ever know about it. It's eighteen years later, and I'm still fighting the damn bureaucracy. We just can't risk any more leaks." He shook his head. "Whatever happened, it was before we left Orand, and that was out of our control. Maybe the King mentioned the plan to a servant who mentioned it to someone else. Or maybe someone overheard, or maybe Kailyn said something when she shouldn't have. I don't know. What I do know is, none of that matters now. What does matter is that Spock, McCoy and Kailyn are going to be in trouble, and that Klingon ship playing tag with us for three days was a trick that I fell for. Now, instead of getting to Sigma as fast as we can to see that nothing happens to the shuttle crew, we have to sit here thinking of a way to wipe egg off Star Fleet's face. *Dammit.*"

There was no easy banter when Kirk gathered Scott, Sulu, Chekov, Uhura, and Security Lieutenant Jaye Byrnes in the briefing room. The situation was summed up in succinct terms, and the assembled officers circled gingerly around it for better than thirty minutes. Finally, Kirk swiveled out of his seat and began pacing around the table.

"Ladies and gentlemen, we're not getting anywhere," he said flatly.

Byrnes cleared her throat. She was present because she'd joined the *Enterprise* after five years in Star Fleet Counterintelligence, and Kirk hoped her expertise might elicit ideas from the others.

"As long as this spy's on board," she said, "we're in control, sir. That's our ace."

"That's what I tried to tell Star Fleet. That's why this shouldn't be that urgent."

"For H.Q. it is," Chekov said glumly. "And that makes it urgent for us."

Kirk allowed himself a gallows smile. "Chain of command, Mr. Chekov. They put the heat on me, I put it on you."

"But who do we put it on?" Sulu grumbled.

"You don't. You give me answers. Byrnes?"

She tossed her blond hair over her shoulder. "We can use that control, Captain."

"How?"

"By giving the spy enough rope to hang himself."

Kirk sat on the edge of the table, arms crossed. "Go on."

"We know about him. We know he's here—"

"Aye," Scott said, "but not who he—or she—is."

"If we can make him think he can get away with something he wants to do and we should normally want to prevent, we might be able to trap him."

Scott nodded. "Aye. Give a fish a little line, let him think he's free . . . he tires himself out, and y' reel him in fast."

"Exactly," said Byrnes. "Now, what would this spy want very much to do, either personally or as part of his assignment?"

"Get away from us," Sulu suggested.

Kirk's eyes narrowed. "Get away from us for what purpose?"

"For his own safety," said Uhura.

"Or to report new information," Scott said suddenly. "Like the King's death. It's the one thing that's happened since we left Orand that the Klingons would want t' know."

"Of course," Sulu said, nodding emphatically. "Then they wouldn't have to worry about getting their hands on the Crown. With the King dead, if they could kill his daughter, they'd wipe out whatever chance we had for keeping the Loyalist Coalition together—"

"—and the Mohd Alliance could win without any blatant outside help that might attract the attention of the Organian treaty enforcers," Byrnes concluded.

Kirk nodded. "That seems like a pretty compelling reason for this informant to want to make contact with his superiors. If we can give him a chance to do that, under the guise of some legitimate task, we could catch him in the act."

"But the only way to do that," said Byrnes, "is to let the spy off the *Enterprise*, sir. And any way we do that, we risk two things—making him suspicious, or letting him escape."

The brainstorming picked up speed and went on for another hour. Kirk was pleased that his inclusion of Byrnes proved to be the perfect catalyst. But for all the ideas laid out, it remained for Kirk to synthesize the possibilities into a course of action that sounded plausible. He did, radioed it to Star Fleet, and waited for an answer.

An hour later, it came: *approval*. But the toughest decision lay ahead. If the hidden spy took the bait, all well and good. But if no suspect stepped forward into the noose, Kirk knew he had no time for alternatives—the *Enterprise* would be off to Sigma in the warp-speed wink of an eye, and to hell with Star Fleet's wounded pride. That could be repaired easily enough—wounded bodies, however, were another matter, and he wanted very much to retrieve the Galileo and its crew unscathed.

But first, to catch a spy. . . .

# Chapter Eight

McCoy twisted in his seat, stretched every muscle in both legs, massaged the kinks out of his neck, and still couldn't get comfortable. Though he'd traveled in space for years, there were still times when he felt slightly cramped walking through a narrow corridor on the *Enterprise,* or sitting in a cabin where the walls contoured to the curves of a bulkhead.

But if the great starship caused a twinge of confinement now and then, three days in the *Galileo* made him feel positively claustrophobic, and he longed for the relative roominess of the *Enterprise.* Suddenly, he leaped from his seat and paced as wildly as a man could with only two strides between him and the walls. Quite frankly, he felt ridiculous and flopped back into the seat. Spock watched without a word, while Kailyn napped in one of the three hammocks set up in the makeshift sleeping section at the stern.

"Spock, are we there yet?"

The Vulcan came as close as he ever did to looking annoyed. "Doctor, you asked me that an hour ago. We are now one hour closer to our destination."

McCoy extended his recliner seat to its full tilt and clasped his hands behind his head. "Tell me again how our destination is a South Sea isle, with palm trees, and suntanned bathing beauties wearing nothing but long, flowing hair, flower necklaces, and warm smiles."

"Sigma 1212 is the fourth planet in its system, sparsely inhabited, and has an average surface temperature of minus twelve degrees Celsius. Sixty-two percent of its landmass is too cold for human habitation. And there are no palm trees," Spock replied, with a suitably icy undertone in his voice.

"You know what I've always liked about you, Spock?"

"What, Doctor?"

"The way you always go out of your way to make me happy."

"Doctor," Spock said, his lips in a tight line, "do one of your crossword puzzles."

"I did a whole tape of them. And I don't even *like* crossword puzzles," McCoy mourned. "What if I said I wanted to go outside for a little stroll?"

"This is hardly the time."

"That wasn't my question. What would you do?"

"At this point, Dr. McCoy, I would let you go."

"There you go trying to make me happy again."

McCoy's next complaint was soundly shaken back from the tip of his tongue when the shuttle bucked into a sudden pocket of turbulence. He grasped the arms of his seat and sat bolt upright, while Spock spun back to the control panel. The ship shuddered again.

"What's wrong, Spock?"

The next jolt threw them against their seatbacks.

"It's getting worse," said McCoy, blanching as his stomach returned to its rightful place, contents barely contained.

The first officer studied several urgently flashing readouts, though his expression remained calm, as always.

"I'm afraid our situation may get considerably worse before it gets better. The Sigma system is noted for the severity and frequency of solar flares and resulting magnetic storms."

"Don't give me a travelog—just do something."

Spock turned his full attention to the *Galileo*'s unresponsive instruments while the small ship tossed from side to side. McCoy stumbled forward, clamping a stranglehold on the command seat's headrest. He hovered behind Spock while his knees absorbed the pitching and rolling.

Kailyn half-fell and half-walked into the main cabin, finally reaching the relative security of her portside seat. "What's wrong?"

"Spock didn't mean to wake you up." McCoy tightened his grip on the headrest. The shuttle's nose suddenly dipped and his chin jammed into the top of the seat.

Dazed, he retreated to his own chair and rubbed his jaw.

"We are entering the storm zone surrounding Sigma 1212," Spock said to Kailyn.

"Surrounding the planet?" repeated McCoy. "That means we're close to it."

"We are approaching it, Doctor, but I've been forced to reduce our speed, and we have another hour ahead of us."

Before McCoy could say anything else, the *Galileo* rose up on its tail and plunged forward as the convulsive fury of the storm jerked it like a puppet. The metal hull groaned and creaked, and Spock cut back the engines again. There was a lull, for just a heartbeat, and then it began all over again. The ship seemed to be trying to twist in three directions at once.

"Spock," said McCoy anxiously, "are we going to hold together?"

The Vulcan's long fingers poised over the controls, and he did not turn to face McCoy. "I do not know, Doctor. Only time will tell."

The Klingon spy vessel shivered and twitched in protest as Commander Kon tried to hold it on course. Kon was short and stocky for a Klingon, but his tunic fit tightly across his barrel chest, and muscles rippled under the mail cloth. His beard was streaked with gray, a telltale sign that he'd been in the Empire's service longer than most, combining skill and luck to survive battles and sidestep assassination attempts by younger officers eager to rise through the ranks. Kon had led the crew of the fiercest battle cruiser in the Imperial fleet for nearly a decade, and had managed to crush a half-dozen mutiny outbreaks to keep his ship loyal to the Emperor. For his efforts, he was rewarded with elevation to the elite Special Intelligence Group, a handful of trusted soldiers who were assigned only the most important spy missions— the dirtiest and most dangerous.

Kon had proven he could kill when he had to, could strangle a child with his bare hands if that's what it took. He was feared, and had no fear. The perfect Klingon.

"Commander, sensors are impaired," said the science officer from her station. The scout ship was tiny, with too much equipment crammed into far too little space. Kera, the science officer, was close enough to touch her commander, though she didn't dare. She was young, brilliant, ambitious—and she knew that any sort of romantic involvement with a powerful male like Kon would likely end up with one of them dead. Not that the prospect didn't intrigue her; for among Klingons, even love was a battle, consummated only when one was victor and one vanquished. But she had time on her side—the odds told her that one day Kon would falter and die because of it. To become too closely allied with him now could cost her dearly later, so the transitory pleasures and excitement of a sexual coupling simply weren't worth the risk.

"We've hit the fringe of a Magnitude Seven disturbance, sir," she said, her voice a businesslike monotone.

Kon's grizzled eyebrows lifted in unison. "Magnitude Seven? And the Federation ship?"

"They've entered it, Commander. We're losing sensor contact."

Cheeks puffed out, Kon thought over the possibilities. "Would they enter such a storm merely to trick us?"

"That would be foolhardy," said Kera. "And their unchanged course leads to the conclusion they're unaware of our presence. In additon, they've exchanged no radio transmissions with any Federation outpost or ship since they left the *Enterprise*."

"So you believe that planet in the middle of these storms is where they're headed?"

"Yes, sir, I do. The Crown of Shad must be hidden on Sigma 1212. I propose that we maintain vigilance outside the storm zone. If they survive to reach the planet and the Crown, we'll have no trouble taking it from them and dispatching the crew when they leave the surface to meet the starship."

"And if they never make it to this treasured Crown?"

"Then," said Kera smoothly, "I see no reason to risk *our* lives by following them into a Magnitude Seven disturbance."

Kon gave her a leering nod of approval, and as she turned back to her screens and dials, he smiled to himself. He wondered what she would be like as a sexual partner, and wished momentarily that he had her back on his warship, with his private quarters. Klingon crew members, whether male or female, had to accept as fact that a commander of the opposite sex had the right to collect carnal favors at whim. And as he looked ahead without enthusiasm to a protracted wait here at the edge of Sigma 1212's violent veil of space storms, he regretted not being able to while away the idle hours getting to know Kera more intimately.

"Sensor contact lost, Commander."

As if the outlying turbulence hadn't been bad enough, entry into Sigma's atmosphere offered no respite. Despite his best efforts, Spock was fighting a losing battle against cyclonic gales of over three hundred miles per hour as the shuttle's outer skin began to heat up.

McCoy had resumed his spot leaning over Spock's shoulder, while Kailyn tried to batten down whatever might be loose inside the cabin. But the time had come to strap themselves in and hope for the best.

"Are we on target, Spock?"

"Difficult to say, Doctor. Instruments have yet to return to normal function. I can only judge by our heading before navigation corrections became guesswork."

"You're not instilling confidence in me."

"You have my sincere regrets. Please secure your safety harnesses. This landing is not likely to be smooth."

Kailyn bit her lip nervously, and McCoy noticed.

"Spock has a way with understatements," he said.

McCoy didn't know how true that really was just then, for only Spock was aware that the whirlwinds buffeting the *Galileo* were making it nearly impossible to keep the heat shields properly angled. *Where* they landed on Sigma might never be a problem—it was quite possible they and the battered shuttlecraft *wouldn't* land, but would burn up in the swirling atmosphere of this planet that seemed determined to permit no visitors.

# Chapter Nine

Trust. If James Kirk held a value sacred, that was it. Without it, existence could never be more than a haphazard series of encounters filled with caution at best—fear at worst. A being deemed unworthy of trust by others, or unable to find fellow-creatures to rely upon completely, could never know true love, unshakable friendship, or the warming shelter of security. In his own experience, lives had been saved by trust, loves lost by the lack of it.

In his eyes, the sin of betrayal was the worst of all. To willingly, knowingly accept someone's trust and then turn against it was contemptible. It was that feeling deep in his heart that allowed Kirk to tolerate for the moment Star Fleet's order to unmask the turncoat in King Stevvin's small, ragtag band of servants.

Four servants, no longer young, their lives given in the employ of the King for thirty years or more. These four had volunteered to leave their home world with their exiled ruler, and in the hard years that followed they had come to feel less like servants and more like members of the family. They'd shared hope and frustration, love, and finally trust—until one of them had betrayed it.

But who? And why? The second question nagged at Kirk. Was it a loyal retainer driven to treason by some weakness of character—an offer of money, or safety—or simply a hollow despair of ever returning home? Or were they dealing with a professional spy, planted in the King's entourage as a matter of course many years before the forced exile?

As he sat at the briefing-room table facing the four

Shaddans, Kirk wasn't sure which answer would make him angrier, and he tried to set such emotion aside until it could be unleashed at a definite target.

Eili, the King's personal manservant. A little round man with the eyes of a faithful dog—once vigilant, seeing to his master's needs even before he would be asked, now dulled by grief. His doughy face was buried in his hands as his wife Dania comforted him. They were a matched set—Dania, the royal cook for thirty years, was as plump as her husband, and as devoted to him as he had been to the King.

Boatrey, the sturdy stable master, his leathery face etched by years of outdoor work. He had been Kailyn's favorite, and Kirk remembered how he would give the little girl rides on the small animals in his stable yard.

Lastly, Nars, the once-elegant chief of the household staff. His clothing was shabby now, with small threadbare spots that had been carefully stitched to get through the lean years on Orand—but he still bore himself with the straight-backed dignity he had displayed without fail in the long-gone days of grandeur.

An unlikely group from which to ferret an enemy agent. Kirk found himself ready to rule out the possibility that any one of them could have been a spy from the start, and he drifted back toward the human-frailty theory. That was why Lieutenant Byrnes was there—her trained eye might catch a hint that he would miss. Kirk cleared his throat.

"Before he died, King Stevvin asked me to promise that he would have a proper Shaddan funeral. I made that promise, and I want to keep it. But we never got the chance to talk about it before the end. I know you've all suffered a great loss with his passing. I share your grief—but right now, I need your help in fulfilling my promise. I need to know the funeral customs of Shaddan religion."

Kirk glanced furtively at each face, hoping to spot a telltale glimmer in the nervous batting of an eye or the downturned corner of a mouth. But if any such sign slipped out, he looked for it in vain.

"We must get a m-m-memorial urn," Eili said, jowls shaking as he tried to control his quiet sobs.

"Is it a special urn?" Kirk asked.

"Y-yes. It must be newly cut stone, quarried n-not

more than a day before death. It . . ." Eili began to weep again, and Nars reached out to touch the little man's shoulder. But Eili seemed not to notice.

"Stone is symbolic of strength, Captain," Nars said. "It must be cut and sanctified according to strict laws."

"I fear we shall not succeed," Boatrey rumbled. "The King's ashes must be set out in the urn, to be sifted and taken by the gods within two suns after the heart has stopped. Aren't we more than two days from home?"

"Three days," Kirk said. "Does the urn have to be cut from Shaddan rock?"

The servants looked at each other before Dania answered. "Not as long as the laws are followed. But who would know Shaddan laws away from home?"

"A Shaddan," said Nars.

"Do you know a planet where we could get a holy urn?" asked Kirk.

"I know of some, but I don't know if they're close enough to your ship, Captain Kirk."

"Let's find out," Kirk said. He reached for the computer terminal and switched it on. The machine's lights blinked in sequence, then supplied a visual response to his query—planets within two days of the starship's present location, with known populations of Shaddan citizens. The servants read the list, and Nars pointed to one name.

"Zenna Four. I lived there myself many years ago."

"But is there a stonemason there?" asked Dania.

"I knew of one. A neighbor."

"But that was long ago," Boatrey protested. "He could have moved on, or died."

"He had a son, who was learning from his father."

"We must try," Eili said. "Otherwise, we condemn our King to wander forever, never being taken to the bosom of the gods."

"But what if this stonemason can't be found?" said Boatrey.

Kirk raised a hand to silence the cross-discussion. "The promise was mine—and the decision will be, too."

The servants were escorted back to their quarters by security guards, while Kirk and Byrnes consulted the computer again. Zenna Four was almost two days distant, closer to Shad and farther from rendezvous with the *Galileo* at Sigma 1212. That meant the *Enterprise* would get back a full day late.

"If the Klingons are still trailing the shuttle," Byrnes said, "and the Crown is found, they could attack before we arrive, sir."

"Let's hold that aside for now, Lieutenant. In your opinion, is Nars the chief suspect?"

"Because he was the only one to step forward and point us to a particular planet? Well, if he is our spy, then he'd certainly be eager to report that the King is dead. They'd probably want to assassinate Kailyn immediately, even if the Crown stayed lost forever. Finishing the Dynasty that way could be quite enough to tip things back over to the Mohd Alliance."

At the same time, according to the computer, Nars was telling at least a partial truth. He had lived on Zenna briefly, as part of a diplomatic mission in a provincial capital called Treaton before he became chief of the King's staff. Zenna had been one of the first planets to contract for tridenite delivery, and a fair-sized community of Shaddans had sprung up to administer the business. The ore trade had dried up by the second decade of the civil war, but many of those Shaddan expatriates remained rather than return home to their own embattled world. So Nars's stonemason might very well be there. Perhaps he *was* only being the dutiful servant to the last, concerned solely with performing this final service for his dead master, sending him on his journey to life after death.

If that was the case, then the detour to Zenna would fulfill Kirk's promise to Stevvin; but it might also place the *Galileo* in grave danger and risk losing the Crown to the Klingons. Though he wasn't religious himself, Kirk knew the Shaddans were. And if he didn't allow the King to be cremated according to custom, how was he to know he wouldn't be depriving his old friend of life after death? He'd already deprived him of almost twenty years of life *before* death. *No—that's not fair . . . not your fault.*

Besides, Kirk refused to believe that the Shaddan gods could be so unforgiving that they wouldn't accept a soul whose delay had helped preserve the Dynasty they'd helped to create. He felt sure that the old King would have agreed with his judgment, and that particular worry subsided. Just one more question before he could choose a course of action. . . .

* * *

"Captain, someday y're goin' t' ask, and my poor bairns'll just give up the ghost. Y'can only ask them to do so much."

Kirk sat on the edge of his bunk and looked at the dubious face of his chief engineer on the viewscreen. "I have faith in you, Scotty. They always listen to you."

Scott sighed. "Aye. We'll gi' you what we can."

With the pledge of extra speed from the starship's well-tended engines, they'd be able to arrive at the Sigma rendezvous less than twelve hours late, and Kirk knew he had to take the risk. He called Nars and informed him that the *Enterprise* was headed for Zenna Four. Nars assured Kirk he'd beam down himself to see to all details. With that, Kirk thanked him and switched off the intercom. He wondered how the *Galileo* was faring.

*There's the rope, Nars. If you don't string yourself up with it, I may have to take your place. Because if I'm wrong about all this, my Star Fleet record may not be worth a counterfeit credit.*

# Chapter Ten

Gingerly, McCoy moved one joint at a time, starting with the pinky on his right hand. When the right hand registered that it was fully operative, he slowly reached up and felt his head. It, too, was operative—and slightly bloody. He opened both eyes completely for the first time since they'd closed themselves up, and a backlog of impressions flooded out of his subconscious. The acceleration, the heat, the nauseous sensation that went far deeper than the pit of his stomach. The expectation of the sound of tearing metal, and quick but painful death, harshly enveloping senses already stretched to the breaking point.

But that last part must never have happened, because he was quite certain he was alive. He gradually realized that he was alone, however, and the floor was tilted at a crazy angle, the craft's fore tip aimed approximately skyward, the stern resting over on its left corner. Debris was scattered across the interior, pieces of equipment broken loose from their moorings and storage niches, the hammocks torn off the wall hangers. He reached for the safety release on his harness and found that it was already unlatched. Then he saw the bloodstained cloth on his lap. It had evidently been placed on his forehead and slipped off. Whoever put it there must have had a good reason, so he put it back, remembering the cut he'd discovered himself a moment ago. That was when he noticed that the wound had been bandaged.

McCoy closed his eyes again, trying to quiet the throbbing that announced itself forcefully along his right temple, slightly below the cut. Where were Spock and Kailyn?

The shuttle door creaked—its track had been bent in the crash, and it resisted sliding back up into the hull. A blast of frigid air rushed in as the door cracked open and Kailyn clambered inside. McCoy relaxed and grinned at her as she wrestled the door closed again.

"You wouldn't smile if you saw what you looked like," she said. Gently, she touched the right side of his head with the cloth. He clenched his teeth at the bolt of pain shooting through his skull and down his neck.

"My head may be split open, but I can assure you my nervous system is working just fine."

"I'm sorry." She pulled her hand back. "Did it hurt?"

"You might say that."

Kailyn bowed her head. "It's my fault you got hurt, and now I'm torturing you, and then I'll—"

"Hold it, hold it," he said, with as much energy as he could muster. "Now, listen here, young lady; you are the only thing that stands between me and this massive headache. Get my medikit and—"

Kailyn held the black pouch up. "Got it already."

"Good girl. There's a small vial labeled 'Topical Anesthetic.' Take it out and open the cap." While she followed his instructions, he winced with another stab of pain. "Now, spray the side of my head with it."

Touching the nozzle with her fingertip, Kailyn lightly dusted the mist over the injured area, and McCoy displayed visible relief as the numbing substance quickly took effect.

"Florence Nightingale would be proud, Kailyn. By the way, where's Mr. Spock?"

"Scouting the area."

"Did he take a phaser?" asked McCoy with sudden concern.

"Of course."

"Oh, good. He doesn't always. Vulcans aren't too keen on killing unless it's absolutely necessary—and what most people might consider necessary, Spock doesn't always agree with." He reached up and touched his head near the gash, then looked at his fingertips. "Well, it stopped oozing. You did an excellent job of first aid."

She blushed. "How do you know I did it?"

"Oh, just a guess. Speaking of guesses, where are we?"

"Mr. Spock wasn't very sure of that."

"Oh, great. If he actually admits to that, then we must

be in real trouble. It felt cold when you opened the door."

"It is. Mr. Spock says it's five degrees Celsius."

McCoy noticed that Kailyn was wearing one of the *Galileo*'s thermal "second skin" jumpsuits, shiny and tight-fitting. "What's the terrain like? I couldn't help but notice we didn't exactly land on a tabletop," he said, gesturing up toward the front of the cabin. He could see gray sky through the front viewing port.

"We're in a valley. Nothing special about it. Oh, there's a river nearby, so at least we have water."

"How are you feeling?"

She shrugged. "Oh, all right, I guess."

"No reaction?"

She shook her head.

McCoy smiled. "That's good. You remember what I told you about being under stress."

She thought about all they'd been through, and her face lit up. "I guess that *is* pretty good."

"Damn good," said McCoy. "We'll give you a shot in a few hours."

The door slid open again and Spock climbed in. "Ah, Dr. McCoy, I see you've regained consciousness."

"Yes, and I see you've managed to get us into quite a fix with your blasted piloting. I told Jim he should've sent somebody along who knew how to fly this thing."

"I also see you've regained your agreeable personality."

"Never lost it. So what do we do now? Where in blazes are we?"

"As nearly as I am able to determine, we are on the correct continent—"

"That's great aim, Spock."

"—within perhaps one hundred kilometers of the Kinarr Mountain range where the Crown is hidden."

"That's not that far off," Kailyn volunteered.

"I wouldn't want to have to walk it," said McCoy.

"For once, you and I agree, Doctor. We are to rendezvous with the *Enterprise* outside this system in less than four days. And there would appear to be no way for us to traverse the distance here within that time."

"What's the difference?" said McCoy glumly. "We can't get off the planet anyway."

"Can't the shuttle be repaired?" asked Kailyn.

Spock shook his head. "Not without spare parts. Not even the communications system."

"So," said McCoy acidly, "the facts are, we're stranded on this planet, we can't get to the Crown, and we can't get to the *Enterprise*."

"Our immediate concern," Spock said, "is survival. Assuming the ship returns to meet us according to schedule, they will not find us, and they will effect a search here on the planet. Our automatic distress signal is operative. If we can stay warm and fed, we can expect assistance to arrive. Captain Kirk is notably punctual."

McCoy brightened. "So all we have to do is tuck ourselves in, close the door, and hope no one knocks till the ship gets here to pick us up."

Kailyn and Spock exchanged glances and McCoy's eyes darted from one to the other. "Why do I get the feeling you haven't told me something I ought to know?"

Spock clasped his hands behind his back. "A substantial portion of our food supply was contaminated. Fluid from various components leaked upon impact. But there is vegetation nearby, despite the rather cold local environment. We should be able to gather a sufficient amount. Kailyn and I will—"

"Hold on, Spock. I'm not staying here all by myself while you two pick berries and nuts. As long as we're stuck here, I'd at least like to stretch my legs. Besides, you're no gourmet—you need me out there."

"Very well, Dr. McCoy. Put on a thermal suit and join us."

Where Orand had been a planet that seemed oblivious of the creatures living on its sand-scoured surface, not caring who or what might stay there and try to endure the heat, Sigma 1212 was quite another matter. Like a wild beast that refused to be saddle-broken, it was vigorously, openly hostile; from the violent radiation belts cloaking it in space to its tempestuous atmosphere, this rock-world bucked and howled and skittered to keep civilization from gaining a foothold amid its sullen valleys and forbidding peaks.

In fact, Sigma's desolation was one of the prime reasons Stevvin had chosen it to hide his Crown. He knew it would serve to discourage casual attempts to search out the concealed icon. Unfortunately, the planet's inhospitable nature could not be peeled aside for Spock, McCoy, and the King's daughter.

Hunched over to cheat the wind's ice-pick edge, the trio moved away from the shuttle wreck. The ground was hard beneath their feet, and not a ray of sun penetrated the curtain of clouds stretching to every horizon. Sigma seemed painted in shades of gray. Even the hardy plants and bushes looked dull and colorless as McCoy and Kailyn broke off berries and leaves that might be edible. Spock dug out roots, checked everything with his tricorder, and carried the food collection in a shoulder bag. If their meals for the next few days wouldn't be especially tasty, at least they would be nonpoisonous.

McCoy scanned the general area, hoping to see some small animals they might be able to capture and cook. His stomach growled uncomfortably and refused to be pacified by thoughts of fibrous vegetation soup. But he spotted nothing furry and footed on the ground; they walked along the edge of a forest zone that extended for at least a half-mile, and he couldn't see anything scurrying among the branches, either. Mixed with the continuous moan of the wind, he heard the rush of water over rocks.

"Spock, let's head down to that stream. Maybe we can catch some fish."

The Vulcan nodded and led the way down a slope covered with grass laid flat by the current of the breeze. McCoy and Kailyn carefully followed. The stream was no more than thirty feet across, and it flowed steadily though not especially fast. Perhaps twenty feet up from the water's edge, the bank angled more steeply; the grass stopped, giving way to hardened mud, rocks, and gravel, and Spock knelt to investigate furrows etched into the ground.

"Fascinating. These appear to be caused by flowing water."

McCoy shuddered. "You mean that little stream gets up this high? What could make it rise like that?"

"Any number of factors. Heavy rains, runoff from the mountains, tidal effects. Meteorological reports on this planet do indicate a high incidence of severe cyclonic low-pressure systems. Such high winds and intense precipitation could account for a rapid increase in water levels of such minor tributaries."

Involuntarily, McCoy glanced up at the clouds, looking for signs of a storm; there were none apparent, but some-

how that made him feel no less uneasy. "I don't like being marooned here, Spock."

"Nor do I. But while we are, there is little we can do,
except to stay alert."

Kailyn stood up straight, turning her face into the wind.
"I don't know if I'm just imagining it, but it feels wetter."

"I think you're right," McCoy said. "We better get back
to the shuttle."

Spock stood and hefted the shoulder bag. "Very well.
We have enough for now. Perhaps it would be safer to observe the weather from a place of shelter for a while."

With that, he took one step up the hillside—and froze,
his slitted eyes sweeping the trees along the upper bank.
Without lifting his gaze, he whispered back to his companions: "Walk down here along the stream bed. I believe we are being watched from those woods."

Grabbing Kailyn by the wrist, McCoy swallowed hard
and silently followed the first officer back toward the
clearing where the shuttle waited.

The stream seemed to be flowing more strongly now,
and the spray coating the waterside rocks made them
slippery. Spock set a rapid but careful pace, and kept one
eye on the trees looming above them.

When they reached a bend in the stream, where the
woods grew down the bank and right up to the water,
Spock made a sharp turn, cutting ahead of who or whatever was shadowing them. He offered Kailyn a hand to
help her make the steep grade more quickly. They heard
a pair of crisp *thwangs*—and two arrows neatly split a
tree trunk no more than a foot from McCoy's head.
Kailyn gasped; McCoy stared first at the splintered tree,
then at Spock. But before anyone could speak, the mysterious trackers stepped out of the gloom of the deeper
forest. Eight humanoids surrounded the shuttle party
without a word or sound. All were seven feet tall or over,
clad in brown and black fur cloaks with animal-skin leggings and boots, their massive heads almost completely
covered by matted hair and beards. One hunter, with silver hair, stood taller than the others; he uttered a growl,
and his band frisked their prey and relieved them of
phasers, tricorders, packs, and communicators. McCoy
and Kailyn remained motionless out of fear, Spock out of
extreme caution; their hands were bound with leather

thongs and they were roughly pushed along a trail through the trees—heading away from the shuttle.

"I don't know what time it is," McCoy whispered to Spock, out of Kailyn's hearing. "But she's going to need a shot soon. Without it, she may not be alive in four days."

Spock stumbled as one of the hunters shoved him. "The same may be said for all of us, Dr. McCoy."

# Chapter Eleven

Spock flexed his wrists, testing the strength and tightness of the woven leather rope binding them behind his back. The pain as the rope bit into his skin was merely distracting, not critical, but it made it clear that the bindings were there to stay.

He, McCoy, and Kailyn were tethered by short lengths of rope to a stout post in what seemed to be a village square, in the center of about two dozen animal-hide tents. The post was designed with deep notches through which the ropes were tied. Had no one been guarding them, Spock might have been able to free himself, but they were being watched by one hunter, the one with the wild silver hair and the girth of a giant redwood. No one in the village was small—even the females were generally a head taller than Spock—but this hunter was among the largest. Judging by the bows with which he was greeted by passersby, he appeared to be some sort of clan leader.

The *Galileo* party had been leashed to the post over an hour ago, almost immediately after the hunters had brought them into the village. The ropes weren't long enough to permit them to sit, so they remained on their feet. Kailyn was tiring, and she leaned alternately on Spock and McCoy for support.

Activity in the square began to pick up. Crude wooden benches were dragged out of tents by perhaps a score of villagers, both male and female, and vending stalls were set up. Some displayed furs and articles of clothing, others stone and wood tools, still others baskets of roots and berries, even vegetables and fruit that appeared to be garden-grown. Villagers not involved as sellers began to mill about the edge of the square. After several minutes, a wizened old male, skin hanging loose like an oversized coat on his rawboned frame, ambled to the center of the grassy marketplace. He had a drum cradled in the crook of one long arm, and he turned his wrinkled face up toward the clouds, mumbled a few words to himself, then beat the drum three times with his fist. At that signal, shoppers spread out and vendors began calling out repetitively, hawking their wares.

As the unlucky group from the *Galileo* watched, they realized that they were the only live goods on offer, and they did not seem to be in great demand. Villagers with other products clutched in their arms and draped over their backs seemed to be giving the silver-haired hunter a wide berth. When a male and female finally wandered too close, he leaped from his tree-stump seat and accosted them with the zeal of a born salesman, chattering in a guttural language that was completely alien to Spock, who listened closely.

The customers were obviously reluctant, and they tried to edge away, as the female tugged at the male's hairy shoulder. But the hunter would not be denied his full pitch, and he clamped a vise grip on the male's wrist. With his other hand, the big hunter scooped up a fair-sized tree branch, almost a log, though in his grasp it looked more like a twig. He dragged the couple closer to the merchandise, and he prodded McCoy with the end of the branch, poking him in the side. The doctor tried to twist away, and his motions seemed to delight the hunter, brightening his face as he spoke ever more excitedly. But the customers remained unimpressed.

The hunter swung the branch over Kailyn's head and stabbed Spock in the ribs. The Vulcan winced momentarily but braced himself and stood stock-still. The hunter did a double-take and glared at Spock. He prodded him again, and his eyes flashed in anger when the captive refuse to budge. With a growl, he raised the branch and cracked it like a whip across Spock's shoulder. Spock closed his eyes, moved his shoulder just a jot—and the tree limb splintered with a sound like a rifle shot. The broken piece flew off end over end, and the hunter stared in disbelief at the stump left in his white-knuckled fist.

The male and female stood back in wide-eyed awe, then realized this was their chance to escape and scuttled quickly to the next stall.

The silver-haired hunter cast a rumbling sneer at his human livestock, shrugged, and tossed the last bit of tree branch off into the brush. Then he resumed his seat on the tree stump.

"How did you do that?" said McCoy in a whisper.

"Temporary suspension of pain input, and a simple exercise of muscle control," Spock answered quietly.

"Could I learn that?"

"I doubt you could sustain your interest over ten years of Vulcan *Kai'tan* classes, Doctor."

"Probably right. Anyway, it's not all that often that someone tries to break a tree over my shoulder."

McCoy peeked back at the hunter, whose anger at losing a sale had subsided. "I don't know if I should be happy or sad that no one seems to want to buy us."

A dirty band of children had been making its round of the marketplace. The hunter took notice as they approached his captives, but only his eyes moved. They ventured closer, these squat miniatures of the village adults, clothed in hide britches. But they stayed carefully out of reach of the small hairless creatures tied up for barter. Even the youngest children had hair on their faces, though less than the adults, and less again on the young females. They stared at the naked-faced ones with eyes narrowed in suspicion—what if the strange ones kicked or spat, or even bit?

One female, as tall as Spock, waited until the hunter's attention had wandered back to seeking out potential buyers, then reached out a fuzzy hand and pinched Kailyn, who yelped. The big hunter sprang to his feet with a roar that sent the young ones scattering like buckshot. Arms crossed over his barrel chest, he gave the merchandise a look, then turned back to his tree stump.

"Isn't that nice," McCoy said in a low voice. "He doesn't want us bruised."

Suddenly, Kailyn slumped and Spock tried to catch her on his hip. The ropes tying them to the post were too short to allow her to fall to the ground, and she dangled, semiconscious.

"She's having a reaction, Spock. She needs a shot of

holulin." McCoy peered into her half-shut eyes. "We've got to have that drug."

Spock turned a rapid look toward the hunter. "Even if he could understand us, he does not seem disposed toward treating us any more kindly than he is at present."

"We're his stock. If one of us dies, that's less he'll get for having captured and kept us. He's got to understand that."

Spock nodded. "They do seem to have a clear comprehension of the rules of the marketplace. In fact, it is quite fascinating to observe such a clearly defined though rudimentary capitalistic system in a—"

"Forget the economics lecture, Spock." McCoy swallowed and faced the huge hunter, without the slightest notion of what to say. He spoke the first words that popped into his head. "Hey, sir . . ."

Spock gave him an arched eyebrow. "Sir?"

"Well"—McCoy shrugged—"it couldn't hurt to be polite."

"I hardly think he'd notice the difference."

But the hunter did notice the attempt at communication. He stirred, raised himself to his full height, and came over to his prisoners, looking more curious than angry.

McCoy felt his heart racing, and figured an extra shot of adrenaline was just what he needed to get him to continue talking to this mountain of a humanoid looming over him.

"She's sick. The female . . ." He pointed at Kailyn's limp body slung against the post. "She's ill." He let his own head slump onto one shoulder in a mock faint, but was sure he wasn't getting through.

The hunter furrowed his brow, leaned over, and picked up Kailyn's head by the chin. He let it go and it fell back onto her chest; he seemed to understand that something was amiss, and he called to a younger, brown-haired male passing by. He was almost a head shorter than the silver-haired hunter, but with his dark mane and beard, and shoulders as broad as a mountain, he resembled a great bear on its hind legs. And he carried a spear.

"A metal-tipped spear, Doctor," Spock noted.

"So what?"

"That means these tribesmen have had some kind of contact with a more advanced culture."

Discussion was cut short by a growl from the old hunter,

and the bear pointed his spear menacingly at the captives while the hunter released the leather thongs from their notched post. He held them securely and shook them like reins to get the prisoners moving. The spear carrier brought up the rear, keeping his eyes and weapon trained on them as they moved toward an unoccupied tent. Spock glanced at the sky—night was coming, and the wind that had settled down to a breeze was whipping up again, making the tents flap in a percussion chorus.

The hunter led them into the tent; there was an overpowering stench inside, and McCoy almost tried to back out—the glinting tip of the spear convinced him otherwise. The old hunter reached down into a dark corner, picked up a small animal carcass and tossed it out, his only comment a grumbling syllable that could have been an oath. The spear carrier kept up the guard as the hunter exited and came back a few moments later with a heavy stone-headed sledgehammer and three horseshoe-shaped posts, larger in diameter than a man's fist. Somehow, the wood had been soaked and curved, the ends sharpened into ground-penetrating stakes. The hunter hammered each one into the soil, then tied his captives securely to them. Once again, Spock, McCoy, and Kailyn were shackled, though at least this time they were bound in a sitting position. The hunter and spearman stepped out, then ducked back in long enough to toss several fur blankets onto the prisoners. The hunter's head drooped onto his shoulder, imitating McCoy's fainting demonstration, and he and his spear-carrying friend left amid growls of something like laughter.

Very little light came in through the slit in the tent flaps, and they shifted their bodies around, trying to arrange the blankets in a fashion that provided both warmth and a little padding atop the hard ground. McCoy shook his head.

"I feel like such a jackass, thinking they'd understand."

"You tried, Doctor."

With his legs, McCoy managed to get Kailyn propped in a more comfortable position, using the curved post as a backrest. Spock offered some help, and together they succeeded. McCoy cocked his ear and listened to Kailyn's breathing; it was becoming labored, with a bronchial rasp. Her eyes were almost closed, and she looked at McCoy helplessly.

* * *

"Spock . . . are you awake?"

"Yes, Doctor."

It was almost completely dark in the tent now. Spock estimated that they'd been there almost five hours, and what sun there had been had long since set. They could barely make out shapes in the chilly dimness, and they could hear that Kailyn was asleep.

"That's good," McCoy said quietly. "At least she's conserving what strength she has left, and the cytotic reaction progresses more slowly if metabolism is slower."

"Then your endeavor to communicate with our captors did indeed accomplish something. We might not have been moved in here had you not attracted the hunter's attention."

McCoy appreciated Spock's attempt at reassuring him, but decided to change the subject. "What was it you started to say about that spear this afternoon?"

"Just that it was steel-tipped, and indicated some contact with a culture more technologically advanced."

"It might just mean they killed some hunters from another tribe and looted the bodies."

"Perhaps. But commerce seems to play an important role here, so it could indicate that they trade with others who live in this region. Since we have seen no means of locomotion other than footpower, it may also mean a more advanced settlement is not far away."

"If it's within walking distance for our friends here, it'd be within walking distance for us."

"Precisely."

"At the moment, however," McCoy said glumly, "something is keeping us from walking."

"Be patient, Doctor. I am presently working on that problem."

The silver-haired hunter was in a foul mood as he shoved the overcooked leg of a small animal into his seasoning pouch, containing gravy made from a spicy root. With one ravenous bite, he stripped the leg of its meat, and the gravy dribbled down his beard. He looked at the gray-brown bone, angry that it contained so little to eat, and tossed it over his shoulder.

In the rest of the torchlit dining tent, villagers ate and talked, mostly in groups; but the hunter ate alone. He had been certain someone would barter for the three creatures his clan party had found in the river forest. The two males could probably work, especially the mysterious-looking one with the pointed ears—the one that had miraculously showed no pain when clubbed with the tree limb. How could such small, frail things have such strength?

McCoy peered into the darkness, trying to make out just what Spock was doing, as the Vulcan raised himself up and sat on the crosspiece of the post he was tied to. From that position, he was able to hook his fingers around it, and he tightened his grip, though the rough wood drove splinters into his skin. For a few minutes, Spock simply rocked back and forth against the post, shifting his weight from back to front, then side to side.

"What are you doing?" asked McCoy. "You don't actually think you're going to pull that out of the ground. You saw the way he pounded that hammer."

"I am not questioning the skill with which our captor wielded his hammer, Doctor. But strength and skill must yield in turn to physical laws."

Spock paused, sat back on the ground, and placed his feet on the crook of the post, puzzling McCoy even further.

"Are you trying to break the wood?"

"What's going on?" said a sleepy new voice in the darkness. It was Kailyn. McCoy's attention shifted from Spock to her.

"How do you feel?"

"Hmmm? Tired . . . weak . . . I guess. What's going on?"

McCoy shrugged, then realized she probably couldn't see him clearly enough. "I'm not sure."

Spock continued thrusting against the wooden post with his legs, alternately pushing and kicking quietly, his boot heels making a slapping noise against the wood.

"It'll never break, Spock."

"That is not my intention."

"Then what is?"

"Whatever went in must come out, given sufficient time and application of force. In addition, this ground is cold. Cold has a consistent effect on many materials, making them contract, and these stakes have been in the ground for several hours now. The chilling effect of the surrounding soil may be sufficient to have reduced the diameter of the wood—"

"And loosened up the posts," McCoy finished. "Theoretically."

"Theories must be tested."

The hunter desperately wanted a sharp, metal-tipped spear, like the one his friend had gotten in trade with the mountain herders. Were not three naked-faces worth *one* shiny-tipped spear? He savagely bit a bone in two, and immediately regretted his fury—the bone had cut his cheek. He spat out the fragments along with a mouthful of his own blood.

The tiny female, though small as a child, might be able to tend gardens or pick berries. He growled to himself and cursed the wind gods for his bad luck. It wasn't often that live creatures were captured and brought back for sale. None in the past year. Perhaps it had been so long that his neighbors had forgotten how good it was to have a slave, if only for trading with other tribes and villages. Meanwhile, he had himself *three* slaves for which he had no use. He would have to feed them, if he ever hoped to sell them, but he barely had enough food for himself, his mate, and their two young ones. The slaves were so small and thin, they probably contained little good meat, but little was better than none. If no one bought them tomorrow, he would have to kill them for food.

Spock shifted to his knees and gripped the post; hands still behind his back, he began working it carefully from side to side. Slowly, ever so slowly, he felt movement— not imagined, but quite real. The lateral jiggling gave way to an infinitesimal yielding upward. He rested, tensed the muscles and tendons in his wrists, arms, and shoulders, and locked his raw fingers around the wood again. He breathed deeply. McCoy and Kailyn were silent, as if their concentration might augment Spock's strength. He coaxed the posts in tiny circular motions, rubbing them against the holes in which the stakes were so snugly contained. Tentatively, he switched the motion, testing, then applied every muscle fiber and ripped upward. He felt the strain, grimaced, and grunted involuntarily. The wood groaned, creaked, and suddenly broke free. Spock lurched forward, falling on his side. He rolled over and stood, holding the post in his hands.

But those hands were still tied behind him.

"Now what?" asked McCoy.

"A moment, Doctor."

Spock bent over, slid his hands below his buttocks, and steadied himself. One foot at a time, he stepped over behind his hands. When he straightened again, his hands rested just where he wanted them—in front—and he soon had the complex knot untied.

"That's much more workable. Now, to the business at hand," Spock said, flexing his fingers to restore circulation.

"Was that a pun, Spock?"

"I don't believe so," said the Vulcan as he bent over Kailyn's restraining post.

The hunter looked up to see his bearlike friend, *two* shiny-tipped spears in his hands! So—he'd traded for another, and now he wanted to look at the naked-faced ones again. Maybe they could work out an agreement in the darkness. The old hunter forgot his anger, for nothing made him happier than the chance to trade. Almost as an afterthought, he grabbed a sackful of roasted legbones to feed the slaves, and he and the spearman left the tent with a torch.

When they came outside, they pushed their cloaks up around their faces, for the wind gods were blowing frigid air down from the mountains this night. The torch flickered, but stayed lit in its shield. There was a warning moisture in the air and they hurried to the storage tent. The hunter threw open the flaps and stuck the torch in ahead of him. He let out a roar of rage—the naked-faces were *gone*. But his friend calmed him—no need to search tonight. There was a storm coming. They would look in the morning light and most certainly find the escaped slaves. Oh, they would be dead, but at least they could be cooked the next night for the tent meal. The silver-haired hunter might not get his spear, but supplying food for the village would get him credit in the marketplace.

Sigma 1212 had a moon—two, in fact—and the same stars that shone on other worlds twinkled in the sky here. But the perpetual cloud cover effectively blocked all celestial light, and Spock, McCoy, and Kailyn were forced to make their way through the frigid woodland in pitch-blackness. The wind blew steadily now, bending smaller trees and twisting limbs on larger ones. The whistle of the wind and moaning branches completely covered any noise made by three cold people fleeing along the overgrown trail.

If they were being followed, their trackers were not close. Spock was fairly certain of that, but of greater concern was finding shelter. Daybreak was too many hours away; there was no precipitation yet, but the chilled air hung heavy, laden with moisture waiting to fall. And Kailyn had to be half-carried by the two men. She was wrapped in a fur blanket stolen from their prison tent.

The search for a haven was imperative, and led them away from the one route they knew—the path along the river that would lead back to the shuttlecraft wreck.

"The three of us will not make it," Spock said.

They rested in the lee of a massive tree trunk crooked over the path after years of trying to grow straight against the ceaseless push of the wind.

"But the *Galileo* isn't that far," McCoy said, hunching over Kailyn to shield her with the warmth of his body. "It only took a couple of hours when they caught us and took us to the village."

"But we had already strayed some distance from the ship, and the hunting party had the distinct advantage of knowing the shortest route between destinations. We do not."

"What do you suggest? We can't spend the night out here in the open. It's either that or pushing on back to the ship."

"Negative. I recall some hills nearby when we were attempting to land."

"I thought you were busy with the controls, not looking at scenery."

"At the time, the hills were an obstruction, not scenery," Spock said stiffly, "and I noticed them while avoiding hitting them."

"Oh . . . sorry."

"At any rate, they were some distance away from the river, but they may offer shelter in the form of caves. That would seem our best choice at this time."

McCoy and Spock lifted Kailyn again. She was conscious, but unable to walk without help. "It's a good thing you're light, young lady," McCoy said.

She smiled weakly—then felt a droplet on her cheek. "Raining," she whispered.

McCoy and Spock began walking as briskly as they could.

The forest began to thin out, and the trees no longer acted as a protective screen. But neither did they block the path with low-hanging branches, and the trio managed a quicker pace. The hills were as Spock remembered them—rocky, covered with a sparse coat of flaxen grass that clung in the face of the omnipresent wind, the force of nature before which all life on Sigma seemed to bow.

The cave's opening was a crevice in the rock face of a low cliff. Without a light or weapon, McCoy had infinite misgivings about entering, even though Spock would go in first. Getting attacked by a creature in its lair would not help matters in the least, and McCoy toyed with discarding the whole idea. Outside, at least, the elements were the only things that could do them in. Inside? An active imagination could conjure up an endless array of fates he would prefer not to meet even in daylight, much less in the confines of a dark burrow.

"What if it's only two feet high in there?" asked McCoy through chattering teeth. He wasn't sure if the chattering was caused by cold or fear. The occasional raindrop had become a swirling mist during their search.

"Since sounds echo inside, Doctor, it is quite likely larger than you suggest."

"Then something probably lives in there. If it has large teeth, I don't want to be an unwelcome guest."

"We shall announce our presence first." Spock picked up a large stone near his foot and tossed it through the cave opening. It clattered along a wall and rolled to a stop.

McCoy held Kailyn tighter; she was barely awake and her head rested limply on his shoulder. Spock kept one ear cocked into the cave, while McCoy found himself holding his breath. No other sounds came out. They waited. Spock threw another rock. Another clatter. And more silence from inside.

Spock looked at McCoy. "It would appear to be uninhabited."

McCoy swallowed. "Either that, or some very annoyed animal is just waiting to sink its teeth into whatever threw those rocks."

"Wait here. I shall be out momentarily."

"I hope so," McCoy muttered.

Spock hefted a sturdy branch as a club, crouched, and disappeared into the cave mouth. McCoy listened, reassuring himself that as long as he heard muffled footfalls and the tapping of the stick, everything was just fine. But he braced himself for the sudden shriek or roar of an enraged beast. *There goes that imagination again. . . .*

It seemed like hours, but Spock emerged about three minutes later. "I do not expect you to enjoy the night in there, Doctor, but it does seem to be safe."

Once again, Spock bent low and led the way in. Very reluctantly, McCoy followed, making certain Kailyn didn't crack her head on any rock outcroppings. He tried to open his eyes to look around the cavern—and then realized they'd been open all along. He couldn't see a thing.

"My god," he whispered, "this must be what it's like to be blind."

"There is a nearly complete absence of light here," Spock said, more by way of information than agreement.

"Then how do you know there's nothing lurking in the corners?"

"I traced the entire perimeter with the stick. In addition, my senses are somewhat more acute than your own —I saw and heard nothing. And this cave is but a small chamber, with no other openings."

"Are you sure?"

"Reasonably."

McCoy clicked his tongue nervously. "You could've said you were *absolutely* sure."

"That would have been untrue."

"You could've *humored* me."

"Enough discussion, Doctor. I shall go back to the ship now and bring back Kailyn's drug and other essential supplies."

McCoy reached out and clamped his hand on Spock's arm. "You're kidding, right?"

"No."

"I never said anything about staying in this cave *alone*." McCoy made no effort to hide his fear.

"You are not alone—you are with Kailyn. She needs

you as much as she needs the drug. You will be relatively safe here. Meanwhile, I will be able to get our supplies much more rapidly alone." There was genuine concern in Spock's voice, and McCoy sensed it. It calmed him—a little.

"I guess I'm supposed to be logical here, huh?"

"That would be a welcome change of pace."

McCoy smiled in spite of his very real anxiety, and he was momentarily thankful for the darkness—perhaps Spock hadn't seen the grin, and he wiped it away quickly.

"Well? What are you waiting for—daylight? Get going, Spock." McCoy felt the stick being pressed into his hand; he suddenly realized he was still holding Spock's arm, and he let go.

"Get some rest, Doctor."

"Fat chance."

"Then keep an eye on the cave entry."

"And if I see anything come in that doesn't have pointed ears, I'll clobber it with this," McCoy said, grasping the stick.

"The animals here may have pointed ears."

"Not like yours." McCoy wiped his palms—despite the cold, he was sweating. "Be careful. And *don't be late.*" There was a shadow across the faint bar of light coming in the opening—McCoy thanked the stars there was that much relief from the blackness. "If you think we're going to wait all night for you to get back, you've got another think coming. Spock . . ." But he knew Spock was gone.

McCoy busied himself with making Kailyn as comfortable as possible. As he started to fold the blanket into a sleeping cocoon for her, he realized that their bodies were the only available source of heat; also, the closer they were, the more readily he could detect any changes in her condition. He found a waist-high boulder in the middle of the cave—by smacking into it with his knee—and decided to use it as a backrest. He propped Kailyn against the boulder, with one fold of the fur blanket as a ground cover, then slid down next to her. The rest of the blanket neatly covered both of them, and he put his arms around her, leaning her head on his chest.

"If only this was someplace else," he murmured with a sigh. "Well, I can't be that old if I can still get a pretty girl to go camping with me."

He smiled to himself as he recalled the days of courting

young girls when he'd been young himself, and the stories his Granddad and Great-Granddad used to tell of their own romantic exploits. Oh, there'd been all manner of social upheavals and sexual revolutions and trends that came and went. But the feelings between a boy and a girl hadn't changed that much over time, even over centuries. In the Georgia hills, the old customs held their ground.

McCoy had met his wife at a square dance the summer after his first year in medical school. They'd walked down the road that led away from the old Simpson barn, on the dust and gravel still warm from a day filled with sultry July sunshine. By the time they'd reached the cool sweet air of the woods and sat on the bed of pine needles and kissed, he'd suspected he might be in love. Across the hills, they'd watched the freighters and shuttles lift off, headed out to orbital stations around the globe—that had been their excuse for the walk, that and getting away from the noise and bustle of the dance—but the launches weren't all that frequent, and they'd had lots of time to chat and spark.

*There was a great old word—sparkin'.* He sighed again, and remembered where he was now. *What's it all worth in the end, anyway?*

He looked down at Kailyn, who snored gently. He could just make out the profile of her face, silhouetted against the inky gray of the cave opening. He kissed her forehead, his lips barely brushing her skin.

Then he heard a howl outside, and a scuffling noise over the rocks. His hand tensed on the stick, but he did not move.

# Chapter Twelve

There was no escaping the rain and sleet that pelted down through the trees as Spock made his way back to the stream. The wind had escalated to gale force, with gusts bending supple tree trunks double; branches were transformed into lethal whips, lashing at anything in their path.

Spock's face and hands were already cut, and the thermal jumpsuit layered on top of his uniform had been slashed as well, letting the rain seep through. He was soaked to the skin. But following the stream trail was his only sure way of finding the shuttle, so he pressed on, protecting his face as best he could.

They had first come upon the stream less than sixteen hours ago, though it seemed like days. It had been a brook then, burbling through the overhanging forest. Saplings had crept their roots toward the water's edge to drink. But the saplings and the banks sloping up into the woods were gone now, submerged under torrents of white water. The gully, where Spock had knelt to examine rills in the cold soil, was completely filled by the surging current. Even the forest floor where he walked was drenched. Puddles were linked by rivulets, and the nearly frozen ground could drink up little of the flood. The footing was treacherous, and it was all Spock could do to keep from falling. He moved to the edge of the woods, walking just above the river's rushing waters. Spray kicked up to mix with the wind-driven rain, and freezing drops swirled all around, burning his eyes.

He didn't see the rock—it was hidden by an ankle-deep pool. But his right boot found it. His heel hit the rock and skidded. By sheer reflex, he grabbed a slender tree trunk on his left as his body fell in the opposite direction. Momentum threw his full weight down toward the river, but his left hand held tight. The tree bent, snapped, but didn't break. The pain in his shoulder almost made him cry out; somehow, he clung to the tree and the roiling waters hissed past him, seemingly in anger at having a sure victim snatched away.

Slowly, holding the tree for support, he got to his feet. His left arm dangled at his side for the moment, and the numbness there was punctuated by a sharp, recurrent twinge. He couldn't decide whether serious damage had been done, but for now he would rely solely on his right. With careful steps, he moved on through the forest.

The howl had only been the wind, and McCoy let himself doze on and off. Even on this wild planet, he had to guess that nature had endowed its creatures with a sense of survival that would keep them all safe in deep, dry places on such a night. It was unlikely they'd have hostile visitors, for only a thing with a penchant for suicide would wander out in this storm. Suicide—or desperation. He could only pray that in Spock's case the second would not become synonymous with the first.

McCoy's eyelids were fighting to close, but he refused to accept sleep at this moment, though he wasn't sure why.

*Sure I know why . . . I don't want to wake up dead.*

"That's stupid," he whispered to himself. "You wouldn't wake up at all. Good grief, I'm talking to myself. . . ."

Dead. *Never really got used to death.*

Lightning crackled outside, flickering through the cave opening with a ghostly glow. Seconds passed, and the delayed thunderclap rumbled over the hillside.

He'd wondered all through medical school whether facing death would ever grow easier. Oh, in some ways it had. After his first clinical encounter with a cadaver, McCoy hadn't quite made it to the sink before he'd vomited the eggs and muffins he'd had for breakfast. In the years since, especially out in space aboard the *Enterprise,* he'd dirtied his hands with more than a score of gruesome deaths, examining crewmen for whom the mysteries of space had included mysterious ways to die. He didn't throw up anymore. Not even the slightest urge. He didn't know if that lack of reaction was good or bad, but it made life a hell of a lot easier—and neater.

Autopsies, deciding cause of death, filling out those damnable death certificates. It had all become routine. It was almost as if the end of a life wasn't final or real until recorded in a data bank somewhere, placed in a computer for easy recall. *Modern man's contribution to the funeral rites.*

The years had made other people's deaths a shade more acceptable, if only to protect his sanity. But his own demise—*that* was quite another matter.

A harsh question drove itself relentlessly into his thoughts: would he and Kailyn ever see Spock alive again?

Finally, McCoy's eyelids closed, and he drifted into a netherworld of fitful sleep. . . .

*. . . Fog hovered everywhere, a spectral veil, shifting with the winds but never dissolving. It hung thickly over the cave opening as Spock approached. The science officer moved slowly, his feet seeming not to touch the ground. Anguish contorted his face as he struggled to reach the cave, arms flailing, slicing the fog as if swimming through it. He floated down, into the cave, and saw two bodies ripped and shredded beyond recognition. From the bottom of a reservoir of suppressed emotions, the hidden fears and dark corners of his Vulcan life, Spock screamed with an agony that went deeper than the soul . . . then he turned and saw the fangs gleaming in the darkness. The creature sprang . . .*

*. . . and McCoy stumbled out of the forest, clothing tattered, skin raw and torn, a growth of stubble on his chin. He was alone. In the clearing before him, the shattered wreck of the Galileo sat, burning. And though he couldn't see them clearly, he knew that the bodies of Spock and Kailyn were in the flames as well. They were dead, and this was their pyre. . . .*

. . . Sweating, McCoy wrenched his eyes open with a suddenness that hurt. He shook his head to wipe out the flaming image that had just seemed so real he could feel its heat. He was breathing as if he'd sprinted a mile, and he estimated his racing pulse at over a hundred. But he was still in the cave, and the only warmth was Kailyn curled next to him.

So, fears of death could still produce nightmares. He held Kailyn close and stared into the darkness.

The shuttlecraft had been cruelly treated by the wind. Not only had the atmospheric maelstrom caused it to crash, but the nighttime gales refused to let it rest in peace. The ship had been tossed like a toy from the rocky perch where it had landed, and it had rolled over an embankment; now, it was almost belly-up, with the door angled down toward the soaked ground.

Spock stood, hands on hips, surveying the hulk. He crawled under the nose, then slithered snakelike through the cold surface mud. Mud. That meant the ground had thawed slightly. Was the air temperature rising? Encased in his wet clothing, Spock couldn't judge.

The shuttle door had been torn open by a boulder, and Spock lifted himself up into the cabin. His eyes made a slight adjustment, and he scanned for things they would need for survival. Only one system still functioned on board—the sealed emergency beacon. He found the medical pouch lodged against the command seat. Spare communicators had been smashed, but the weapons cabinet in the bulkhead was intact and he took four phasers out. Food concentrates. Two hand-sized electro-lanterns. A spare tricorder. Maps of Sigma. A tent packed in a pocket-size pouch. Laser flares.

Spock sealed the supplies in an unbreachable pack and hoisted it over his good shoulder. The injured left one felt slightly improved; at least it was mobile again, though he was sure a thorough exam would find something wrong. That, however, was a luxury that would have to wait.

He glanced quickly around, decided he'd taken everything that might be of use, then lowered himself through the hatchway and slid out from under the *Galileo* on his back. The precipitation, more sleet and freezing rain than liquid now, cut into his face like needles, forcing his eyes shut for a second. He set his mouth in a grim line and ran for the woods, splashing across the flooded clearing.

Spock tried to drive all extraneous thoughts from his mind, saving his concentration for placing one foot ahead of the other as safely and quickly as possible. Anxieties flashed by as single-frame images before they could be quashed by Vulcan self-discipline: McCoy fending off beasts seeking the shelter of the cave . . . Kailyn slowly dying without her holulin injection . . . the *Enterprise* doing battle with Klingon ships determined to undermine this mission.

*Vulcans do not worry*, he assured himself. *We accept what we must. We do what we must, logically.*

He reached the densest part of the forest, and it became apparent that the trail was nearly impassable. Fallen tree limbs, some the size of logs and too heavy to move, crisscrossed the path like barbed-wire barriers. A jagged pair of blue-white lightning streaks split the northern sky and found their mark some distance away. Spock decided to cut through toward the river—he *had* to quicken his pace.

The storm had lasted almost all night long, and showed no signs of blowing itself out. The fury of the sky and clouds powered the river to new heights, and the frenzied water pounded its banks without letup. Stones that had marked high water on Spock's last pass had long since gone under. Oceanlike waves swept high and crashed into the trees just ahead of him, and he braced himself and waited. The surge passed and he took a step. The ground gave way beneath him and a ton of earth and rock tumbled into the river with him. The wave dipped low, poised like a beast to attack, then cascaded over him. He swallowed a mouthful of muddy water, tried to hold his breath, then felt a tug downstream. The equipment pouch was still snagged on his shoulder, and the air sealed inside made it buoyant.

He tried to slip it under his chest, giving him the best chance to keep his head above water and push himself away from rocks jutting into the river's path. But the ride was too rough for maneuvering, and he simply held tight to the pack straps as the current dragged him downstream, away from the direction of the cave, where McCoy and Kailyn waited—and toward the brink of a towering waterfall.

# Chapter Thirteen

The silver-haired hunter had not enjoyed his morning meal. The inside of his cheek was raw where he had cut it the night before, and he was angered by having to get up before dawn to seek the bodies of the escaped slaves. And if by some miracle of the wind gods they were *not* dead, he would surely kill them with his bare hands for all the trouble they had caused him. How much more he would enjoy running them through with a shiny-tipped spear; but he couldn't get one unless he had something to trade, and right now, the slaves were his only goods . . . or *had* been. Therefore, if he did find them living this dawn, he would not be able to kill them after all. He growled.

His bearlike friend squatted on the forest trail. The rain had stopped, and the wind was beginning to dry out the ground. Preserved in the hardening mud were three sets of clearly etched footprints. The big hunter glowered as he looked down at the tracks; he had an urge to smile, but that would only have ruined his terrible mood.

The tracks continued. The naked-faced ones had gone toward the hills, and so did the two hunters.

McCoy rubbed his eyes and convinced them to focus. The cave was still dark, but a shaft of light edged through the entryway. It was morning, though certainly not bright out. Kailyn slept almost silently, still nestled in the crook of his arm. His hand tingled; the arm was asleep.

He tried to shift the elbow without disturbing Kailyn. It didn't work. The moment her neck moved, her eyes opened, blinking groggily.

Spock still had not returned.

"Where are we?" asked Kailyn in a hoarse whisper.

"In a cave."

"I guessed that," she said as she stretched.

"Do you remember last night?"

"Not really. I had a dream about going through a forest in the rain. I was wet . . . and cold. I guess it was more like a nightmare than a dream."

"It wasn't either one. It was real. Spock went back to the ship to get your holulin and some other supplies, and he's not back. I'm worried."

He stood up and started for the cave opening. He heard a pebble roll down the rocky face of the hillside, and he froze. Was it the wind? A wild animal? Then he heard voices, speaking the rumbling, guttural words of the villagers who had captured them. Noiselessly, he reached down and grabbed the stick.

"What is—?"

"Shhh . . ." McCoy tiptoed to the side of the doorway and pressed his back to the cave wall. He held the stick head-high, poised like a gun trigger. He motioned for Kailyn to join him. She left the blanket and scuttled over to huddle behind him.

"At least I can belt *one* of them if they try to come in here," he whispered.

McCoy held his breath and waited. The soft steps of the hunter's boots were barely discernible, betrayed only by an occasional scuff of leather on sand and rock. But they moved closer, no longer accompanied by voices. A shadow cast itself across the cave floor, covering the morning light that shone in dimly. The shadow paused and the scuffing ceased. McCoy could hear his own heartbeat, feel it from his knees to his throat. Kailyn stood frozen next to him, anchored to the floor.

A whining phaser beam suddenly sliced the stillness, the shadows fell away from the cave entrance, and McCoy and Kailyn gasped together as they heard a sound like two filled sacks thumping onto the hard ground. But they didn't move until Spock's head poked into the cave. His face was dirty and bloody, but at the moment, McCoy decided it was good enough for him.

"It sounds to me like we owe our lives to two well placed trees, Mr. Spock."

"How so, Doctor?"

"Without them, you probably would've drowned twice."

"My reflexes and ability to remain in control under stress played some small part."

"Sure they did," said McCoy as he dabbed at a cut on Spock's forehead. "In a pig's eye."

Spock raised an indignant eyebrow. "I could hardly have predicted that the bank would collapse the moment I stepped—"

"If that tree trunk hadn't been skewered between two rocks, you'd have gone over the falls, Spock."

"But I had to have the presence of mind to grab it, Doctor."

"Poppycock. It sounds to me like it practically hit you on the head." Without skipping a beat, he turned to Kailyn. "And how are you feeling, young lady?"

She was resting on the cave floor, curled in the blanket, one of the electro-lanterns near her. "Much better."

"Nothing like a little holulin injection and food to put the bloom back in those cheeks."

Spock sat cross-legged and went through a series of isometric exercises. He was bruised, but entirely functional. The heat of the nearby lantern had dried out his clothing and he felt more comfortable. "Considering the obstacles that have confronted us so far, I would say our condition is satisfactory at present."

"We're all alive and in one piece," McCoy admitted, "but we're also low on supplies, we've got two unconscious cavemen"—he gestured at the hunters tied up and lying in the corner—"who'd love to kill us, we don't know where we are, and we don't know where we're going. I'd hate to see what you call unsatisfactory."

Spock pulled a pair of plastic-coated maps out of the supply pouch. McCoy knelt next to him.

"I believe we are closer to our intended destination than we had originally thought," Spock said. He pointed out several features on the charts, which had been drawn up combining space survey records with details recounted by King Stevvin. "We may be within one day's walk of the mountains."

Spock watched McCoy mull over that possibility, then raised one eyebrow. "You have an opinion, Doctor?"

"Well, we can't stay here. That's for sure," he said, glancing back at the hunters.

"Is Kailyn strong enough to travel?"

"I am," she piped up.

McCoy glowered. "*I'll* make the medical judgments."

"It will be a strenuous journey," Spock said.

"I know, I know."

"We may not find shelter."

"Stop playing devil's advocate—though the ears fit the part. Look, we have the thermo-tent, and it's big enough for the three of us. And if it turns out that we have to stop and camp out in the mountains, we'll be no worse off than we were down here last night. The sooner we get going, the better I'll feel."

Spock raised a questioning brow again.

"Why so surprised?" asked McCoy.

"I expected you to resist the idea of our traveling farther."

"If we had a choice, I would—believe me. If we stay around the shuttle, we'll have to dodge our hairy friends. Oh, sure, the *Enterprise* might find us—but I don't want to be found in pieces. Jim has the coordinates for that mountain stronghold where the Crown's supposed to be. If we can get there and find this Shirn O'tay person, Jim'll be able to track us down. You do think he'll look for us there, don't you?"

"It would be the logical thing to do, and the captain is quite logical, for a non-Vulcan. I should point out, however, that the mountains cover a considerable span of territory. It will not be an easy task to ascertain the Crown's exact placement."

"Hope springs eternal in the human breast, Spock. What about Vulcans?"

"Only logical expectations spring from ours, Doctor."

"Is our getting rescued a logical expectation, Mr. Spock?" asked Kailyn.

The first officer fixed her with his usual impassive gaze. "Perhaps."

McCoy smiled to himself. Coming from Spock, that was practically an admission of hope. For now, it would be quite enough.

# Chapter Fourteen

Nars hated being in a spaceship. He felt boxed in, controlled, like a lab animal. The starship's mazelike corridors increased the illusion, so he'd been staying in his quarters as much as possible. Boatrey had been sharing the two-room cabin with him, but the stable hand was now off eating with Eili and Dania. Nars was hungry, but he knew his stomach wouldn't keep a meal down, knotted as it had been since Captain Kirk told him they were going to Zenna Four.

As much as he disliked the confinement of the ship, the vast emptiness of space was far worse. Nars had always been a man who liked solid ground underneath his feet, with horizons farther off than the mere reach of his hand. He liked to know there were places he could go if he had to—places to seek things out, places to escape things. It was a freedom that worked both ways. A vessel, however large, out in interplanetary space—that was a combination that offered him no solace at all.

He jumped involuntarily when the call came through from the bridge—the *Enterprise* was entering orbit around Zenna Four, and his presence was requested in the Transporter Room.

If there existed a common anxiety among good commanders, it was the fear of being *out* of command. Though experts weren't able to reliably pigeonhole people the way they could the properties of biology and physics, command of people was still a science of sorts. At least, the *approach* had to be scientific and orderly—control as many variables as possible, and command became that much simpler.

Nars was such a variable, and the moment he sparkled out of the transporter chamber, he was free of Kirk's grasp. That thought brought a furrow to Kirk's brow as he sat with Lieutenant Byrnes in the lounge, staring at a cup of tea. Transporter Chief Kyle informed them of the beam-down.

"Well, Byrnes," said Kirk, "it's up to you and Chekov."

"Yes, sir." She left, and Kirk stirred the tea absently. Then he looked down at the cup. He stopped stirring, and the tea continued to circle the cup without his assistance. *Control sure is hard to come by,* he thought.

Nars swirled the sickly greenish drink around the tumbler in his hand. He looked up at the clock over the bar, then took a sip. It was the only watering place in town, but it was still too early in the afternoon for the local farmers and laborers and artisans to be drifting in. It was also too early for his meeting, but he was nervous, too nervous to drink any more. He left a coin on the counter and headed outside.

Treaton had only one main street, and it looked much as it had the last time Nars had walked it twenty-five years before. There had been little growth in any part of Zenna, none since the tridenite shortage began in the last decade. The government could have turned to other power sources in its effort to industrialize, but the Zennans were patient, loyal folk. They had struck a fair bargain with Shad's ore traders, and they would wait to see how the war ended. If the King's Loyalists won, tridenite would again be available. If the Mohd Alliance won, and tridenite remained embargoed, only then would Zenna seek out an alternative. Zennans avoided urgency; the future would always be there and they were in no hurry to overtake it.

*The bird catches its prey, eats it, and it is gone,* went a native proverb. *And what then is left?*

The same brightly painted, high-gabled houses that Nars remembered lined the street, and the residents wore gaily striped togas identical to the ones their parents had worn. Change was not an important process, and life as a whole was easy on Zenna Four. Here in Treaton, the seat of provincial government, strangers were hailed as neighbors by every citizen who passed by. Immigration statutes were as lax as any in the known galaxy, making outworlders like Nars quite commonplace.

It was rather easy to pick out a foreigner—very few Zennans surpassed five feet in height, and skin colors ranged from pale pink to bright orange-red. Men uniformly shaved their heads, and women wore their hair in a single braid.

Just being in a Zennan town made Nars relax a bit— the great tide of friendly greetings as he strolled toward the street's south end pushed worries to the back of his mind. But they rushed forth again as he approached the last house on the right. It was set back from the road, surrounded by tall, broad-limbed trees that screened its windows. Privacy was not highly valued on Zenna Four, but this house seemed built for it. Nars pushed open the plank gate and crossed the yard with its unkempt yellow grass. He rapped uncertainly on the door, and a moment later an old Zennan man swung it open. He wore a simple gray toga, indicating his position as house servant.

"May I help?" he asked in a high-pitched singsong.

"Is . . . is your master at home?"

"Yes, yes. Please enter."

Nars followed the little butler into a dark study. The butler then backed out, shutting the woven wicker doors. As Nars stood uncomfortably, a high-backed desk chair swiveled to face him and a skeletal man stood, with his hand extended out of the shadows.

"Welcome, Nars," he said. "It's been a long time between visits."

Nars took the welcoming hand, but didn't clasp it warmly. "A long time, Krail."

The man stepped into the halo cast by a wall lamp. He was a head taller than Nars, with dark skin stretched tautly over his aquiline face. His gray beard and hair were neatly trimmed, in marked contrast to his bushy, upswept eyebrows. Krail was a Klingon of unusually aristocratic bearing, and Nars felt very much the servant in his presence. He did not like the feeling.

Krail issued a pinched abbreviation of a smile and motioned to a hard-backed chair. As Nars glanced around, he noticed nothing suggesting softness or luxury in the entire room. The floor was bare wood, the windows cloaked by severely drawn drapes, and the furniture angular and uncushioned without exception.

"A drink, Nars?"

The Shaddan nodded curtly. Krail slid open a dark-wood cabinet and took out a sharply sculptured crystal decanter. Smoothly, he poured two goblets of blood-red wine and handed one to his visitor.

"It is, of course, imported," said Krail with cold pride, "from my home world. We Klingons are more than merely great warriors."

Krail's thin smile made Nars most uneasy. He wanted to get this over with as rapidly as possible and he carefully placed his cup on a table and stood. "We have business, Krail. Let it be done," he said, a shade more urgently than he'd intended.

Krail looked mildly disappointed as he pursed his lips and measured Nars with guarded gray eyes. "Is there a hurry?"

"My time with you is not unlimited. Let's leave it at that."

"Ah, yes," Krail said with studied sympathy. "You have the *Enterprise* to worry about. But I think by now you may be safe here, and we'll arrange passage to a Klingon planet, as we promised you. You will—how shall I put it —disappear before Kirk's eyes."

"That won't be necessary," Nars said quickly.

"Oh? Are you severing your dealings with us after— how long has it been?—eighteen years or more?"

The Klingon's tone was vaguely menacing and Nars felt cold sweat break out on his upper lip. All those years had made little difference—he'd never learned to trust Klingons, no matter how much they paid for the information he smuggled to them. Krail's cold smile appeared again.

"Fine, fine. Many ships pass through Zenna. Whatever destination you choose is fine with us. You certainly won't want to remain among the rancid little rodents populating *this* planet."

Tolerance had never been a common trait among Klingons; Nars had noted that many years before, and it always put him on guard.

"Now, to your unexpected information," said Krail. "I must say I was very surprised to be told you were here and wanted to meet with me."

Nars swallowed and felt his neck bob. "The King of Shad is dead."

Krail had looked away, but he turned his head to stare sharply at the Shaddan informer, a rare departure from his usual calculated motions. "Indeed? So, this *is* unexpected information. The Federation has bungled more completely than we could have hoped. Even sabotage could never have been so effective." He began to pace, his long legs striding, mantislike. "Yes, yes . . . this places our entire strategy in a new light. Our objectives can be simplified. All the long years of—"

His words were cut off in mid-thought by a ruckus from the foyer. The butler squealed a loud "No entry!" protest; deeper voices and heavy footsteps flew toward Krail's study, and the wicker doors burst open a few seconds later. Two men and two women entered. They wore the simple hooded cloaks and fatigues of spacers from a hundred worlds—but the weapons they held were readily identifiable. Federation phasers, pointed calmly at Krail and Nars.

The Klingon quickly regained his composure, and the thin smile showed itself again. "You would be considered guests in my home except that *I* do not take kindly to weaponry in the house."

"*You* be quiet and don't move," Lieutenant Byrnes said sternly. "Commander Krail, isn't it?"

Krail looked pleased at the recognition but said nothing. Chekov glanced at Byrnes. "You know who he is?"

"Sure do. He's been around for quite some time. Assassinated about twenty superiors to get where he is today —on the Klingon Intelligence Council, one of the top four spies in the Empire. Which makes me wonder what he's doing out in the field, doing a quadrant commander's dirty work . . ."

"I don't know what you're referring to, uh . . . ?"

"Lieutenant Byrnes, commander . . . of the *Enterprise.*"

"Ahh. I make this my home now. I enjoy this world, with its charming, friendly natives."

Nars shot him a surprised look—from rancid rodents to charming natives in just a few moments. Truly a startling verbal metamorphosis. But Krail ignored the stare—he was too busy dueling with the intruders.

"Nars can tell you I lived here, oh, almost twenty-five

years ago, when he first came to Zenna. That's when we met."

Nars went pale. "I don't know what he's talking about. I—"

Chekov cut the Shaddan off sith a warning glare. "You wouldn't happen to be a stonemason in your spare time, would you, Commander?"

"Why, no," Krail replied innocently.

"I didn't think so. Well, we not only get *this* cossack," said Chekov, nodding at Nars, "but we bring back a jackpot bonus, too."

Security Ensign Michael Howard, stocky and brighteyed, frisked Nars and drew an *Enterprise* communicator out of the frightened man's pocket. He cradled the device in one hand, touched a button on his tricorder, and smiled with satisfaction as the tricorder emitted loud rhythmic beeps. "I think I'll give him a reward . . . maybe replace a few worn chips and spruce him up for next time."

"*It,*" said Chekov irritably. "*It,* not *him.* You sound like Mr. Scott, the way you talk about those devices of yours."

"Watch it, Chekov. Devices have feelings, too," Howard said defensively.

"Should we search the rest of the house?" asked the female guard, Maria Spyros.

Byrnes shook her head. "Krail may not work alone here. We got what we came for—a whole lot more, in fact. Let's not stick around and get into trouble."

"My people will know I'm missing," Krail pointed out

"True," said Chekov, "but they *won't* know what you and Nars know. Ready to beam up, everybody."

The landing party stepped into formation, with its prisoners in the center. Howard flipped open the rigged communicator. "Landing party to *Enterprise.* Standing by to beam up. Energize."

A moment later, they sparkled out of existence, leaving the astonished butler cowering alone.

The *Enterprise* warped out of orbit immediately, bound for Sigma 1212.

Nars broke easily. He was not, after all, a professional spy, and Kirk figured he'd carried his burden long enough. The once-proud servant was almost thankful for the chance to talk. He had indeed met Krail a quarter-century before, during his brief stay on Zenna as a staff member of the ore-trade mission. No deals were made then, and Nars had forgotten the episode—until he fled to Orand with the King.

"Punishment in hell couldn't be worse than life on Orand," Nars whined. There were tears in his eyes and he stopped to wipe them.

Kirk was a compassionate man; he'd once liked Nars, but he found it hard to feel sorry for him now. The captain had to force himself to hold his anger in check, and he let Byrnes conduct the interrogation.

"Go on," she said.

"We were all in despair those first months there. We talked of suicide, all of us taking our lives together. For us, our world had been stolen away from us and we feared we would never return home." Nars paused—for effect, it seemed to Kirk. The Shaddan glanced at the faces of his listeners, hoping to see some melting in the detached hardness of their eyes. "Don't you understand?" he cried.

"I understand what you felt, but not what you did," Kirk said harshly.

"We thought we would *die* there," he blurted, rising out of his seat. A burly security guard pushed him back, gently but firmly.

"You all felt that way," Kirk said. "You were all afraid, but only *you* committed treason."

Nars covered his face. "I was the only one seduced by Krail and his promises and threats."

The Klingon had been a mid-level operative then, charged with subverting the Loyalist forces any way he could. Two months after the royal party had taken up residence in their Orandi country house, he had renewed his contact with Nars.

"He came to the compound with two peddlers."

"What was his offer?" asked Byrnes.

Nars mumbled his answer, ashamed. "Money."

Kirk felt his jaw and fists tighten. "How patriotic."

"You weren't there," Nars said starkly. "We had nothing but four walls. That money let me buy pieces of a life. Not just for myself, but the others, too. I could buy books for the King, and for the Princess. For the Lady Meya, herbs and medicine when she fell sick. Small things for my staff, to make them less unhappy there."

"And what did you sell?" said Byrnes.

Nars snorted a hollow laugh, with a touch of hysteria woven into its texture. "What did I sell? Nothing . . . *nothing*. In all those years, I told them nothing of use to *anyone*. What did I have to tell them? Answer me, Captain Kirk. You were the one who sent us to hell. We rotted there for eighteen years. For all those years, we lived as the dead do, with nothing to mark one day different from the last or the next. *What could I sell them?*"

He leaped from his seat and clamped his hands on Kirk's shoulders, catching the guards off balance. Kirk shoved him down again, and the guards held him belatedly. No one spoke. Nars breathed hoarsely.

"For eighteen years, I told the Klingons about such important state secrets as the Princess's birthdays, the King's despair and sickness, the death of Lady Meya," he whispered bitterly. "I had no military secrets. When I tried to stop, they threatened to harm the King and his daughter. They said they could kill them anytime they wanted, and no one would know or care. I did it to protect the family. There seemed no harm—"

"Until you betrayed a sacred trust and told the Klingons about this mission," Kirk said in a voice of stone.

"What else did you do with your money?" asked Byrnes, steering away from Captain Kirk's barely controlled rage.

Nars collapsed onto the table. "Nothing. I did *nothing*," he sobbed piteously.

"He purchased the favors of women," Krail said carefully. "To put it in delicate terms for you, Lieutenant Byrnes."

"I didn't know Klingons could *be* delicate," she said. "Don't stint on my account."

Krail had taken Nars's place in the interrogation cell. Kirk leaned against the wall, and the pair of guards stood just inside the force-field doorway.

"If you insist," said the Klingon. "Nars is not the most proper fellow he purports to be. It seemed that during his time on Orand, he'd developed quite a few private depredations, including something called pipeweed. I believe one smoked it. He could really get quite desperate if his supply ran out. I suppose you might say he was addicted."

"And how did he get this addiction?" asked Kirk. "Could you have introduced him to it?"

"Captain, I resent your attempt to link me to—"

Kirk cut him off with a fist on the tabletop. "I've had my fill of you, Krail. Nars's fate is out of your hands. As for you, whether you cooperate or not, confess or keep silent, we have more than enough evidence to send you to a prison colony for the rest of your life."

"Not a very enlightened system, Captain."

"Lock him up," Kirk said abruptly. He gave the Klingon a glance of contempt and stalked out of the cell.

Star Fleet would have their spy—with an extra big fish tossed in for good measure. *I hope they're thrilled*, Kirk thought as he made his way to the turbolift on the brig deck. Nars had turned out to be unworthy even of disgust, and one less Klingon spy, albeit an important one like Krail, would not make one whit of difference in the balance of power.

He stepped into the waiting lift. The doors hissed shut behind him and he turned the control handle. "Deck five."

What mattered now was whether they could get to Sigma 1212 in time. All the carefully planned strategy had degenerated into a race against the clock and the Klingons. At this point, Kirk knew he was powerless to do any more than hope that the rush to rescue the crew of the *Galileo* would not become a search for bodies.

The King's body reposed in the sick bay morgue, and there it would stay. There was no stone urn, no proper Shaddan cremation, no entry into the next life. Not yet. If Stevvin was to join his ancestors, he would be late. Kirk hoped the gods would understand, and forgive.

# Chapter Fifteen

The Kinarr Mountains stood like sentinels daring travelers to pass. The lofty range, almost as old as the planet itself, held the Crown of Shad somewhere among its peaks. Had the *Galileo* been able to land at the coordinates laid out by the King, the search would have been short and direct. But as they climbed ever higher on trails spiraling narrowly through perpetual fog, McCoy was becoming convinced the quest was hopeless.

They stopped to rest in a cove etched into the mountainside by millennia of wind and water. For the moment, it protected them from the gusts that alternately tried to pin them to the inside wall of rock rising up from the trail, or blow them over the outside ledge. McCoy gave Kailyn an injection of holulin, then sat on the ground and leaned against a boulder.

"Spock, why are we doing this?"

"You know why, Doctor."

"Tell me again, 'cause right now, I have my doubts. Here we are climbing a mountain somewhere in the middle of a two-hundred-mile range—"

"We know we are proceeding along the most logical course."

"We have no way of knowing if we're twenty feet or twenty *miles* away from that Crown."

With a shake of his head, McCoy gazed out across the Kinarr Mountains; the tops of all but a few were lost in the dense clouds that hung over the whole region. Visibility was limited, but what he *could* see made McCoy distinctly unhappy.

"They all look the same," he moaned. "There aren't a whole lot of landmarks, Spock. We've been climbing since morning, four hours, and we don't know if we're getting closer or farther away. That makes it kind of hard to go on."

"What happened to all your optimism?" Kailyn wondered.

"I left it a few miles down the trail."

"You accurately stated that we had little choice in our present course of action," Spock said patiently. "Debating it serves no purpose whatsoever."

"In my head, I know you're right. But my feet keep telling me you're wrong."

Kailyn stood. "The *Enterprise* will be back here in about two days. I don't want it to leave without us, and the only way we can be sure of being on it is to get to Shirn O'tay's settlement."

She reached her hand out to McCoy and helped him up. Refreshed by her shot and the rest, Kailyn bounded out ahead. McCoy started after her.

"The young lady convinced you rather readily, Doctor."

McCoy gave him a sour glare. "Shut up, Spock."

The difficulty of the climb varied—from bad to worse, as far as McCoy's legs were concerned. The higher they went, the steeper the path wound. Vegetation became sparse, and ice-edged gusts bit through their clothing. Patches of snow appeared with increasing frequency, and soon more of the rocky ground was blanketed than bare. The fog had thickened from a filmy haze to an opaque mist, obscuring even the nearest peaks; after a while, McCoy found an odd comfort in the fact that he couldn't see past the rim of the trail—he was allowed to forget about the steep slope that fell away just a few feet from where they walked. Only an occasional stone kicked over the edge would serve as a fearsome warning, clicking down the rocks below, finally falling out of earshot. It was a long, long way down.

"Eight to ten thousand feet," Spock estimated during their next pause along the trail. McCoy sat flat out, stretching his legs.

"I have so many kinks, I'm going to need a wheelchair,

Spock. Air's getting pretty thin." McCoy rubbed his eyes and sighed. "I'm too old for this."

Kailyn dropped to her knees beside him. "No, you're *not*. This should help." She began to knead his calf muscles and the backs of his thighs. "I used to do this for my father when we went on hikes."

For a moment, a faraway look glazed her eyes, and her massage weakened.

"Don't stop," said McCoy. "What's wrong?"

"Nothing," she replied wistfully. "I was just thinking about Father, wondering how he is."

"Don't you worry," said McCoy, holding her hand. "I may be the chief surgeon, but my staff can do just fine without me."

"Oh?" said Spock casually. "Then why does the captain continue to put up with you?"

"Because I'm such a joy to have around," McCoy snapped. "Come on, let's get going." He grunted as he clambered back to his feet.

Kailyn held tight to his arm. "I have promises to keep, and miles to go before I sleep," she murmured.

"Isn't that from a poem?"

She nodded. "A great poet from your planet—Robert Frost."

"Oh, yeah. A New Englander. I always preferred Dixie poets myself."

The sun of Sigma 1212 blazed forth with a sudden and stunning glory. After the time in space, where giant suns are reduced by distance to twinkling pinpoints, and the past day of doleful clouds and violent storms, it shone now like heavenly fire, flooding the mountaintops and their snowcaps with a blinding brilliance. While they'd been walking, the dense fog had begun to thin gradually with altitude, but the brightening came in increments so small as to go unnoticed by three climbers more concerned with the path under their feet than the sky over their heads.

And so the sun had burst upon them like a celestial flare. Free of the fog, peaks soared wherever they looked, and they stood in breathless awe, perched at the top of this world, surrounded by pristine beauty and whiteness so stark it made their eyes ache. McCoy squinted, refusing to close out the light that made him feel renewed.

"I'd forgotten what sunshine looked like," he whispered.

Kailyn peered down the mountain at the clouds below them. Before, they'd appeared unremittingly gray, but from this new vantage point, they seemed a pure and fluffy white, like a carpet below them. "I feel like I could just leap out there and walk on them," she said, wandering dangerously close to the edge of the trail. She felt giddy, like a child in a wonderland.

Not even Spock could resist the splendor basking before them. Through slitted eyes, he looked from horizon to horizon, momentarily overwhelmed by the sweeping panorama stretched below like some vast artist's canvas. "Incredible," he said in a hushed voice. "Such unspoiled beauty."

"I've never seen anything like it," said McCoy.

Spock scanned down the steep mounains, then back up to the sun, a deep orange-red. The sun. Ever so slowly, it was moving, across the white-blue sky and down toward the horizon. Time passed, unceasingly. Night crept closer.

"We must move on," he said, finally.

McCoy thought he sensed a tinge of regret in the toneless voice of rationality, and he looked directly into the first officer's eyes; he found what he sought.

Spock gazed back, without shame. "Appreciation of great beauty is not illogical, Doctor."

"No, it's not," said McCoy gently.


For a while, the trail seemed to descend, in concert with the sun. Shadows lengthened and crossed their path as Spock continued to lead the way. Once more, they stopped to rest their ever-more-weary legs. Spock, too, had begun showing signs of fatigue, in shortness of breath and obvious stiffness in his left shoulder, the one injured during his ordeal the previous night. McCoy slumped to the ground, near exhaustion, and Spock knelt next to him.

"Perhaps we should make camp here, Doctor."

"No," McCoy wheezed. He glanced out at the sun, which was poised to dip below the field of clouds. "We've still got some daylight left. A little farther."

"Whatever we do today is distance we don't have to cover tomorrow," Kailyn said.

Spock sat alone to consult the maps, while Kailyn stood and turned toward the broad vista, her back to McCoy. He watched her with admiration. A girl—no, a young woman. While McCoy's old legs told him to stay on his backside awhile longer, he knew now that Kailyn was tougher than any of them had thought. Through the roughest stretches of climbing, even when they had to be tied together at the waist by safety cords, she never faltered, never missed a step. He was proud of her, and felt the impulse to tell her so. But not now—later, perhaps when they settled in for the cold night ahead. With greater effort than he wanted to admit, McCoy got first to his knees; then, one leg at a time, he stood up unsteadily. Neither Spock nor Kailyn saw. He tried to take a deep breath, but his lungs protested and he coughed, a rumbling sound from deep in his chest that alarmed him. Kailyn heard it and turned quickly, her lithe body still encased in the skintight thermal suit. Her face flashed her concern in a deep frown—the cough sounded like her father's the last time she'd seen him.

McCoy grinned at her, then nodded toward Spock, who was still with the maps. "You think he's gotten us lost and won't admit it?"

Spock looked up. "We are following the correct route."

McCoy leaned close to Kailyn and said in a stage whisper: "I *told* you he wouldn't admit it."

The trail continued on a downhill slope, and twisted around a bend. Spock suddenly stopped and held up a hand for silence. McCoy strained to listen. There was no mistaking—there were voices up ahead. On this narrow mountain trail, there was no place to hide—and they were about to run into a band of humanoids. The figures were far below, heading up; they looked like snowmen, dressed in white parkas.

"Oh, lord," said McCoy in a low voice, "please don't let these be like the last ones."

Cautiously, Spock moved ahead. "Set your phaser on stun, Doctor."

"I don't like shooting people, Spock," he said—but he set the switch as instructed, and kept Kailyn in line behind him.

"Neither do I, but it is best to be prepared," said Spock.

There was some*thing* sprawled across the path ahead of them; the curve and grade of the trail placed them out of sight of the group of natives downhill, and they approached it warily. It was a dead animal. Its dusty-white woolly coat was stained with blood, presumably its own, and its four legs were splayed out under it. Either it was freshly killed or the cold air had preserved it, for there was no smell from the carcass. As they moved closer, they could see that it had two great antlers, intricately curved, growing from the front of its head. It was a massive beast —at least eight feet long.

"Whatever killed it packed quite a punch," said Mc-Coy. He leaned over to examine a triple slash gouged into one antler. "Looks like a three-toed claw of some kind."

He narrowed his eyes and brushed something off the tip of one antler—a bloody patch of white, furry hide. "Also looks like he took a hunk out of his attacker," he said, slipping the hide into his pocket.

"What a magnificent creature," Kailyn breathed. "It didn't die without a fight."

"Indeed," Spock agreed. "Though it was fatally wounded, it is largely intact. Whatever killed it must have been a carnivore. Odd that pieces were not removed for food."

McCoy peeked over the edge of the mountain. "Take a look down there."

Spock and Kailyn both glanced down. Far below, barely visible, a white animal was grotesquely draped like a gargoyle on a ledge. It looked like a cross between a mountain lion and a bear. McCoy began a comment, but was cut off by a new voice, clearly threatening though it spoke in an alien tongue. Spock, McCoy, and Kailyn turned as one and saw that the way was blocked by the humanoids they'd seen up ahead. Their faces were visible now inside their fur-trimmed hoods—deeply tanned, moon-shaped, with even bangs of jet-black hair. And angry.

There were an even dozen of them, all with steel-tipped weapons—spears, bows and arrows, and long-bladed knives. The leader, burlier than the others, chattered loudly and aimed sharp gestures at the animal carcass.

"We did not kill it," Spock said evenly. He had no idea if the leader understood; for emphasis, he pointed to the gash in the antler, avoiding motions that might alarm.

"We found it here—dead."

The burly Sigman had a silent reply—he pointed his loaded longbow directly at Spock's chest. At a quick nod of his head, his companions surrounded the shuttle party.

They moved with swift agility, showing no fear of the trail's edge or the long fall that awaited the careless.

"I suggest we offer no resistance," said Spock in a low voice.

"Here we go again," said McCoy as their hands were tied behind them.

The setting sun cast long rays through the clouds, painting the skies in vivid splashes of gold, red, and deep blue. The armed group took the *Galileo* crew about halfway down the mountain where a narrow pass cut the one peak into two. The pass was less than thirty feet wide at its opening, but it broadened gradually as they descended, finally flaring like a funnel after perhaps a half-mile. The mountain band finally paused—spread below was a shadowed valley, nestled between the towering Kinarrs. On one side, a deep V of sky separated two mountains; they seemed to be bowing before the sun, permitting it to shine through to the inner plateau. But except for that opening, the valley was completely protected by the encircling range.

The farther down into it they went, the warmer the air got—the winds that ruled the high alpine peaks could not enter here, and the weather was calm.

Only the top sliver of the sun was still visible, and it bathed those parts of the valley it could reach with its crimson radiance. The trail changed into steps carved with great care right into the stony surface of the planet. The steps dove straight down the slope, pausing at wide intervals for small platform landings. At each one was a broad, flat boulder with engraved images on its altarlike top—pictures of animals prancing against mountain backdrops. The leader knelt before each altar on the way down, with the others standing silently, heads bowed, as he offered a prayer. The ceremony was repeated five times.

At last, the steps reached an end, and multiple paths branched off from their base. The sky had turned blue-black, and stars began to sparkle. The ground suddenly rumbled, and an eerie chorus of howls and grunts drifted up from a lower road. Soon, a herd of at least a hundred animals clip-clopped into sight. They walked with a rhythmic gait, driven slowly by twenty of the mountain folk. As they passed, Spock noticed that several of the herders were females, and the animals were the same as the dead beast they'd found on the trail. A musky cloud of dust followed the herd, and McCoy sneezed. When the animals had gone, the captives were led into a cavern.

McCoy stifled a slightly nauseous feeling at being in a cave again, but it wasn't difficult to do—this one resembled the previous night's hiding place as much as a sod hut resembled a Dixie mansion. The opening was low and they had to duck down, but the interior broadened out to a high-vaulted grotto, with ceramic oil-burning lanterns along the walls, and support columns made of carefully fitted stone bricks rising up into the shadows. A massive altar dominated the central room, with stone steps leading to its pulpit fifteen feet up. Painted animal carvings decorated it on all sides.

Perhaps fifty of the mountain people stood around the shrine as one tall old man mounted the steps. He wore white woven leggings and a brightly striped poncho. His hawk nose jutted away from a face framed by flowing white hair and a beard down to the middle of his chest. Taking the steps in ceremonial cadence, he reached the top, where a small animal lay, twitching instinctively as it tried to wriggle free of the leather harness that held it. It was a baby from the herd, a male with the first downy growth of antlers sprouting above its eyes. Tiny hooves clicked against the rock altar, and the tall man drew a gleaming blade of the scabbard at his waist. He raised hands and eyes toward the ceiling far above, and spoke in ringing tones. Spock understood.

"Let the wind gods see us, and sanctify this sacrifice of the Night of Darkness. When the moons shine again, may our prosperity and peace be renewed."

He plunged the knife down and the small beast yelped. Then it was still—the clean stroke had done its work mercifully, but McCoy still felt vaguely queasy. He glanced at Kailyn, who watched the service with wide-eyed absorption.

Two young men, dressed in leggings and vests instead of the heavy outdoor parkas, bounded up the altar steps as the tall man came down. They untied the dead animal and carried it away, down a corridor off the main cave.

The burly trail leader waited patiently for the tall man to get through a knot of people gathered around him. Finally, he came across and stood before the trail leader, who whispered in his ear. The tall man nodded his white head; the others stepped back and he approached the prisoners, regarding them with searching eyes. His face was crisscrossed by tiny lines and wrinkles, like an intricate map etched on old leather. The hawk nose prominently displayed its blood vessels, and the eyelids hung low under extra folds of skin. But there was a calm strength in this face, and the voice swelled with authority.

"Who are you that raid our snowsheep herds?"

Spock lifted an eyebrow. "We did not raid your herds. We found the dead animal on the trail, just as your men did. The snowsheep had been attacked by something with triple-toed claws, and—"

"How do you know this?"

"We saw marks on the antlers, and found this."

McCoy angled the pocket on the back of his thermal pants toward Spock, and the Vulcan took out the patch of bloodstained white fur. The tall man held it up, then turned to the trail leader.

"Did you see the marks?"

The burly man nodded, and examined the scrap of animal hide.

"We saw the attacker dead on a ledge below the snowsheep," Spock said. "It was the color of that piece of skin."

The tall man drew in a deep breath. "A zanigret," he said to the trail leader. "These travelers have been held without need. Release them."

Immediately, the hand ropes were untied.

"You are free to leave," said the old man.

"Now?" asked McCoy.

The old man looked down at McCoy with a curious stare. "Of course, but only the foolish travel in darkness, when the zanigret prowl. You are welcome to remain with us until morning, then go back to your homelands."

"We are unable to return to our homelands," said Spock. "Where we come from is far from these mountains. Before we can go back, we need to retrieve something that was left here by a friend of ours a long time ago."

"What is this thing? Perhaps we can help you."

"Perhaps you can. We are trying to find the settlement of Shirn O'tay. Do you know him?"

The man's eyes crinkled under his snowy brows, and he smiled. "You seek the King's Crown?"

"How do you know that?" asked McCoy in astonishment. And as he asked, the answer dawned on him. "Of course—you *are* Shirn O'tay."

The old man bowed deeply. "Not a day has passed without thinking of the King. Is he well?"

"He is ill," said Spock, "too ill to come back for the Crown himself. This is his daughter, Kailyn."

"Ahh, yes," Shirn said in delight. "The child, the little child. But you've grown so." Shirn shook his head. "To think after all this time and wind has blown over the mountains . . ." He stopped in mid-breath. "Oh, but of course you *do* come from far beyond the mountains. You come from other worlds, other stars. You must rest and eat with us." He clapped his hands and shouted: "Prepare for the Feast of the Moons! Come, come! You will eat on my blanket!"

The old chieftain led his people from the shrine chamber into a smaller side cavern where the feast would take place. Spock, McCoy, and Kailyn followed the crowd.

"We're in the home stretch, Spock," McCoy crowed. "I didn't think I'd live to see it."

But the joyous tide swept Kailyn along in body only—her spirit was troubled. She had been so caught up in the physical trials of reaching the Crown, she had allowed herself to forget the rigorous test that she would have to face alone. Neither McCoy nor Spock could help her once it was placed on her head. The biggest task of her young life loomed nearer than she had ever thought it would, and it made the trek through the terrors of Sigma 1212 look like child's play. She found herself wishing they were still out on the mountain trail somewhere—anywhere but this close to the Crown of Shad.

# Chapter Sixteen

Commander Kon's patience had long since run out. The space storm had kept him from making a close approach to Sigma 1212 for nearly two days, and tensions aboard the Klingon spy scout hovered dangerously close to the boiling point. His hulking weapons officer glanced at Kon uncomfortably from time to time—no doubt the man's jaw still smarted from the punch Kon had thrown in their scuffle that morning.

As a commander, Kon preferred to have his orders obeyed without enforcement tactics, certainly without brawling. But Lieutenant Keast had insisted on giving unsolicited advice. When Kon had warned that he was on the edge of insubordination, Keast had become abusive. The punch had silenced him rather effectively, though upon later reflection, Kon had to admit to himself that he was lucky he'd caught the much bigger and younger lieutenant off guard.

As the hours wore on, he looked at Kera more and more often. Not only did he prefer her beauty to the sullen faces of his two male officers, but she was the one who would inform him of the storm's abatement. Finally, she did.

"Can we move in, Kera?"

"Yes, Commander. Completing preparatory sensor sweep now."

She turned back to her computer console, hands resting lightly atop several control switches, ready to shift modes and readouts. The stream of data meant little to Kon, and he waited, once again with a full reserve of patience.

"Something strange, sir," Kera said with a frown. She touched a sequence of buttons. "Receiving communication from the Federation vessel."

Kon sat upright on his couch. "Is the *Enterprise* within range?"

"Negative, sir. No ships but our own."

"Then who are they communicating *with?*"

"Ahh. No one, it seems. The message just repeated. It's an auto-distress signal."

"So . . . the Federation ship didn't land successfully after all. Our decision to wait was an excellent strategic move, wouldn't you say, Kera?" Kon spoke loudly, his barb aimed at Keast, who slouched in his seat, sulking.

Kera smiled coolly. "Excellent, Commander." Perhaps after this mission, she would reconsider a sexual coupling with him. The look in his eye was unmistakable—the choice up to her. But that was for later consideration. "We are locked on to the Federation ship's position, sir. Landing may proceed."

The Klingon ship set down about a mile away from the abandoned *Galileo,* in a clearing not far from the stream, which ran fast and high within its banks. It was sunset, though the cloud cover made the sky look even duskier, almost completely dark. With a search-lantern beam probing ahead, Kon led the way to the shuttlecraft. Cutting winds swept over the lowland terrain, and all four Klingons held their weapons drawn as they cautiously approached the wreck.

"Any life readings?" Kon asked.

Kera scanned the *Galileo.* "None."

Kon turned to his two male officers. "Stand guard outside while we search the interior."

A gust of wind blew by and the ship's ripped metal hide creaked and moaned. Kon whirled reflexively, his weapon at the ready, then relaxed and looked sheepishly at his science officer. "All this waiting has me a little jumpy."

"Just don't shoot me by accident."

Kon shook his head. "Not you. Keast perhaps."

They both laughed and climbed under the shuttle's flank to get at the doorway. Once inside, Kon panned around with the light beam while Kera turned her sensor toward all nooks and corners.

"No bodies," Kon mused.

"Some blood, though," the science officer said, holding up a dark-brown-stained cloth. "Someone was injured."

They were interrupted by a soft, repetitive beating sound on the hull. "What's that?" said Kon.

"Sounds like rain."

They listened for a few moments, and the beating grew more insistent—harder, louder, faster.

"Commander," Keast shouted from the hatch, "it's pouring out here. The skies suddenly opened up."

"If he gets soaked," Kera said in a low voice, "you'll never hear the end of his complaining. You don't want to have to hit him again, do you?"

Kon made a face of disgust. "Very well," he called. "Both of you come in here."

Keast and his fellow guard clambered up through the jagged opening. They were already drenched, and the chilly air made them shiver. Kon glared at them while Kera continued her thorough reconnaissance of the shuttle cabin.

"Weapons are missing. Most of their food supplies are back here, but they're contaminated, sir."

"Evaluation?"

"I'd say they were able to leave here, but how far they could've gotten is impossible to estimate—especially with the weather conditions on this planet."

"Yes," said Kon thoughtfully. "Federation weaklings would not fare well in such a rugged climate—unlike us Klingons." He glared at his shivering officers. "*Most* Klingons, at least."

"I'm sorry, Commander," Keast protested, "but it's very cold—and getting colder."

"Wherever they are, they're well-armed," Kon continued. "That means they could have attacked any natives in the area to get food and shelter."

"Except that Federation cowards don't operate that efficiently," Kera reminded him.

"When it comes to survival, even a mongrel Star Fleet officer like that half-Vulcan Spock would kill if he had the chance. Keep that in mind, all of you. If we find them, be ready to kill on sight."

"In the meantime, sir," said Keast belligerently, "what do *we* do?"

"We wait out this storm. I'd hate for you to have to get wet again."

"But the Federation spies could be——"

"——sitting someplace, doing exactly what we are—— waiting," said Kon, cutting him off. "We'll be losing no ground. I'm sure they're not far from here, and we'll have no trouble tracking them once the weather improves. You're not as reluctant to travel in darkness as you are in the rain, eh, Keast?"

"No, sir, I am not," said the lieutenant stiffly.

The Klingons spent over an hour in the leaky shuttle wreck, but the rain only worsened. A swirling wind current spun through the forest, ripping up trees and tossing them like twigs. Picking up debris, the storm funnel howled across the flatlands and barreled over the hills. It bore down on the *Galileo* and flipped it like a child's toy being thrown by the hand of a giant.

The Klingons inside never knew what hit them. Keast was killed instantly when his skull slammed into the sharp edge of a split bulkhead. The other male officer was catapulted out the hatch opening and crushed against the boulders below as the wreck rolled over him. Kera and Kon held fast to couches still fastened to the floor, and were both alive when the wind passed and the *Galileo*, broken in two now, came to a stop against a cliff almost a hundred yards away.

They stumbled out into the heavy rain. Kon fell to the ground, semiconscious. Kera held her right arm close to her side, protecting a rib she suspected was fractured. She knelt in the cold oozing mud and used her sleeve to wipe blood away from her commander's eyes——then she saw the deep ugly gash above his nose.

"Can you stand, Kon?"

"I think so. We have to get back to our ship. Help me up."

She did her best, and the two of them limped toward the relative haven of the woods.

"The stream," Kon whispered through bloody lips. "Have to follow it."

"We're almost there."

Kon tripped and fell, grabbing Kera for support. His arm closed tightly around her waist and she cried out in pain——he had found the broken rib. She held her breath, fought back tears, steadied both of them and moved on through the trees.

They could hear the roaring of the water just ahead, though it was barely audible over the screaming wind. But it would be their guide back to the safety of their own ship.

Thunderstorms rumbled to the west. A Medusa's head of tangled lightning bolts ripped across the sky, splitting off and plunging toward the planet below. One struck an ancient tree that towered above the forest trail. The tree exploded and shattered, spraying shards of wood like shrapnel in all directions. Kera shoved Kon down behind another low-hanging tree—an instant too late. A ragged spike drove itself into Kon's chest, and he was dead before he hit the ground. Kera lay on top of him.

"No!" she screamed, then strangled another cry starting deep in her throat. The only answers from the tortured lords of nature that ruled this wild planet were the steady downpour, the thunder, and the crackling of the burning tree stump. The charred wood hissed as the rain hit it and turned to steam.

Kera was alone—but she was a Klingon. She would have to go on and attempt to complete this mission—*alone*. Or die trying.

# Chapter Seventeen

Shirn O'tay proved to be a gracious host. His blanket was actually a sumptuous fur rug made of zanigret skins and padded underneath with the fleece of the snowsheep. The Feast of the Moons marked the simultaneous phasing out of both moons, an event that occurred only four times a year because of the unequal orbits of the Sigman satellites. The darkened skies represented the cleansing change of seasons, and the new moons to come up the next night were worshiped as harbingers of good fortune.

Long platters of meat from slaughtered sheep, and an assortment of vegetables and herbs were welcome sights to the trio from the shuttlecraft—a far cry from the berries and concentrates they'd had over the last two days. They were finally able to peel off their dirty and tattered thermal suits, and afterward McCoy and Kailyn gorged themselves; Spock ate only the herbs and vegetables, and all three listened eagerly as Shirn answered their many questions about his mountain settlement.

"We've lived much the same for hundreds of years," the old man told them. "Our fathers found this valley, and took its discovery as a sign from the wind gods. As you've seen, our world is not altogether hospitable."

"Well, you've certainly made up for the planet's bad manners," said McCoy between bites.

"The storm we encountered in the lowlands—is that a common weather pattern here?" asked Spock.

"For the lowlands, yes. Even for the mountains—but not within the bosom of the Kinarrs, where we are. Here on the plateau, we rarely get more than a gentle snowfall. The snowsheep lived in this valley before our fathers came, and they became domesticated very easily. There is a story we have the children tell at feast times, so the old tales will live on. Tolah! You'll start."

A pixie of a girl rose from a blanket at the far side of the cave. She padded over to Shirn and stood before him. She looked about eight years old, and wore a bracelet of bells that jingled gently as she moved. He handed her a scroll.

"Tolah, the story of the first snowsheep."

The little girl took a giant ballet step away from Shirn and spoke in a serious voice. "The first snowsheep greeted our fathers at the break in the Kinarrs, and he had *big* headhorns, much bigger than nowadays."

She knew the story by heart and continued without even a glance at the scroll. "And he would not let our fathers pass. And the snowsheep said, 'You can't come in here. This is holy land and only holy people can live on it.' And our fathers said, 'We *are* holy. The wind gods told you to save this land for *us*.' And then—"

"Very good, Tolah," Shirn said, his eyes sparkling with pleasure. "Kindrel—you next."

Kindrel, a blond boy of about thirteen, took the scroll and read in careful, dignified tones. " '*Prove* you are holy,' said the sheep. And the First Father grabbed the snowsheep by his horns and they wrestled for four seasons. When the seasons ended, the snowsheep said, 'I am the strongest creature, sent to guard the holy lands. Only holy people can be as strong. You are truly Kinarri—children of the Kinarrs. You are welcome to live with us in peace, and my brothers and sisters shall be your servants.' And that is the story of the first snowsheep."

Kindrel slowly rolled the parchment and gave it to Shirn. The old man nodded proudly. With a ceremonial bow, the boy returned to sit with his family.

Later, the platters were cleared, and candied fruits were brought out along with a sweet, steaming-hot drink made from tree sap. Spock wondered why Shirn's people had never modernized their way of life.

"Because we have no reason to, Mr. Spock. I went away to school when I was a boy. My father sent me to a Federation colony, hoping I might learn something to help our people."

"Did you?" asked Kailyn.

"I learned what we didn't want to be, and that a leader

cannot force his people to change in ways they cannot. We have a small community here, perhaps five hundred of us. The hot springs in the caverns support our gardens, with special lights we bought from traders. The snowsheep provide meat, milk, cheese, manure for fertilizer, clothing, and other supplies. A sheep that dies or is slaughtered is used completely. Zanigret attacks are our only problem, and they occur mostly at night. That's why we keep the herds in the caves at night. The one you found had run off."

"Such economy, applied on a larger scale to a more modern way of life—" Spock began.

"—is very difficult to attain. We are not closed off from the advancements of our age—we adopt new tools, and trade freely when traders come our way. But we seek not to upset our balance, our traditions of all these years."

"It's Shangri-la." McCoy murmured.

"What does this mean?" asked Shirn.

"It's an old Earth legend, about a place high up in the Himalaya Mountains, where things hadn't changed for thousands of years, and people hardly aged. Now, *that's* something I could use."

Shirn gave a rueful laugh. "As you can see, Doctor, we *do* get old."

"Shangri-la was supposed to be a paradise, and that seems to be what you've got here."

"If I may ask," Spock said, "how does your succession of leadership operate?"

"We are a mixture of democracy and dynasty. The oldest child of the late leader takes over—unless a majority votes for someone else. But we rarely have a dispute. For instance, my daughter—Tolah's mother—will follow me when I die."

The conversation, fascinating as it was, with richly rewarding exchanges of information for both sides, eventually turned to the Crown of Shad. Kailyn listened, as she had done most of the night.

"Can we see it?" asked McCoy.

"It isn't right here with us," said Shirn.

"Where, then, is it kept?" Spock said.

Shirn pursed his lips. "In a safe place. King Stevvin warned me that it should not be readily accessible, in case his enemies ever found out where he had taken it.

In fact, *he* doesn't even know its exact location—he left that up to me."

"Well, can we have it tonight?" McCoy asked.

"I'm afraid not. It will take us several hours to reach, and we cannot go until daylight." A troubled look crossed Shirn's seamed face. "Even then, I can't simply *let* you take it."

"Why not?" said McCoy.

"Because I promised the King that only the rightful ruler would be allowed to have it."

McCoy bristled. "Kailyn *is* the rightful ruler. You must believe that."

"In my heart, I believe all you've told me, without exception. But I took an oath. Kailyn must prove who she is."

"Our word isn't proof enough?" McCoy's eyes flashed in anger, and Kailyn touched his hand.

"Shirn is right. I'll have to prove it at home. It's only fitting that I should have to prove it here first."

"How?"

"By showing that I have the Power of Times, that I can master the sacred crystals of the Crown."

Kailyn found Spock after the feast had broken up, in the scroll room, a square cave off the main grotto. There, cabinets full of parchment rolls held the story of the Kinarri herders from their earliest days on the protected plateau. The scrolls were written painstakingly in the hands of as many different scribes as there had been generations of Shirn's people. Carefully drawn pictures and diagrams cropped up often to illustrate tales of hunts and harvests, legends of the wind gods and heroic exploits. With the aid of a set of translation pages, Spock was able to gather the drift of most of what he read, idea for idea if not word for word.

As he read, he recorded the handwritten works on his tricorder after convincing Shirn it would be a terrible loss of history if the parchments were ever destroyed.

The Vulcan looked up as Kailyn sat on the rug next to him.

"Are they interesting?" she asked.

"Quite. It is rare that a society living on such a relatively primitive level should keep such detailed records of written history."

"Usually, they'd just be oral records, right? Passed down from generation to generation in the form of stories?"

Spock raised an eyebrow in mild surprise. "Correct."

Kailyn smiled. "Social history was one of my favorite studies when I was growing up." The smile faded and she looked away. "Growing up. I feel like I'm still growing up."

"That is not unusual," Spock said softly. "I have never understood why so many races instill in their offspring the notion that growing up, as you phrase it, is merely a stage of life that one passes through in a finite period of time."

"Isn't it?"

Spock shook his head. "Perhaps the terminology leads to errors in perception. If it were simply referred to as 'growing,' perhaps it would be easier to conceptualize as a process that continues throughout life."

"That's too logical for most beings, Mr. Spock," she said with an ironic smile. "Most races aren't Vulcans."

"So Dr. McCoy persists in telling me. Instead of devoting effort to becoming more logical, he prefers to avoid it and remain—"

"Handicapped?" Kailyn volunteered.

"I would not use such a strong word."

"Why not? It *is* a handicap, to be caught up in emotions and fears."

"Vulcans have emotions," Spock said carefully. "However, we do not let them interfere with rational observation and judgment."

"I wish I were a Vulcan. It would make it a lot easier to be a leader."

"Not necessarily, Kailyn."

"But I've watched you. You can size up situations, take advice, weigh choices—and then *act* forcefully in a crisis." She sighed, and her eyes were even more sad than usual.

"You are drawing conclusions from incomplete data. You have only observed me in a discrete set of circumstances."

"But I know what I saw—"

"You saw me acting as a leader because I was placed in such a position by assignment of Captain Kirk."

"Do you want to be a captain yourself?"

Spock almost smiled—how often he'd heard that question. "No, I prefer to gather information and deliver it in orderly, usable fashion to those who can best apply it to decision-making. To advise, upon request."

"But you're in command on this mission . . ."

"As a Vulcan and Star Fleet officer, I carry out those duties assigned to me. Captain Kirk is an example from which you might learn a great deal."

"What *makes* a leader, Mr. Spock?"

He paused to consider, and thought mostly about Kirk —the qualities that made him a man others would always turn to and follow. "An ability to delegate tasks, to know subordinates so well and trust them so completely that they can be relied upon to do the job as if the captain himself had done it. In return, they trust him and give their loyalty willingly."

"I didn't mean only Captain Kirk."

"I realize your reference was generic, but I know of no better example," Spock said quietly.

"That's what my father always said." She sighed again. "I wish the captain was here to talk to . . . or my father."

"You might try talking to Shirn O'tay."

Kailyn brightened. "I think I will."

The short, bearded man bounced up and down on his feet, and his gravel voice nearly shouted at Shirn.

"But I swear the buck is *mine!*"

A younger man leaned down, nose to nose with the bearded fellow. "And I say it's *mine*. It came back to the cave with *my* herd—that makes it *mine*."

Sitting on his white rug on the ground between them, Shirn listened patiently, seeking the right moment to intervene. When the bearded man paused for a breath, Shirn spoke up—*quickly*. "At this rate, the buck will die of old age before you decide."

"No it won't—I'll *fight* him for it," said the bearded man heatedly.

The younger herder rolled his eyes. "Oh, gods in the mountains. You always want to fight, Blaye. When will you—"

"Wait, Dergan," said Shirn to the young man, "Blaye has a point. Fighting *is* one way to settle differences."

Blaye planted his feet far apart and his hands on his hips, as if to say, *I told you so.*

"But," Shirn continued, "it's a troublesome way. Even if you win, you're bruised and weary. I remember when I was a young man and I fought over a snowsheep. Oh, I won, but I was so tired, I couldn't drag it back to my herd and it ran away and right into a zanigret's claws."

Blaye shifted his jaw back and forth nervously, softening his bellicose stance a bit. Shirn's eyes shifted from one to the other.

"Are there other ways?" Shirn asked.

"That's what we came to *you* for," the bearded man said.

"Ahh, of course. Well, we could kill the buck and divide it in half."

"Wait," Dergan protested. "That buck will be fathering offspring for years. I'm not going to give up a stud sheep for a pile of meat and bones!"

"Neither will I!"

"Well, then, what about a split of those offspring?"

"Never!" roared Blaye, his voice echoing off the cave walls. "I'll have to wait three Feasts for the first calf. Meanwhile, he's got the buck all that time, and that beast will be into every cow in his herd!"

"Dergan, are any of your cows pregnant?"

"Three of them."

"Answer me this—you didn't have that new buck when you went out to graze this morning, did you?"

"Neither did he! And it has no brand. . . ."

"But *you* have it *now*," Blaye rumbled.

Shirn finally got to his feet. "That's quite true." He towered over both men and placed an arm around the shoulders of each. "What about this? Dergan keeps the buck—"

"No!" shouted Blaye.

"—and Blaye gets the first born from your herd, his choice of buck or cow."

"But that's not *fair*," Blaye said.

Shirn let go of the younger man, and ushered Blaye to a corner. "If anything, *you* get the better of the bargain, my friend. He gets a beast well along in years, while you get one that's fresh and healthy with a whole life ahead of it. Hmm?"

Blaye scratched his beard as he thought about it. Meanwhile, the old chieftain ambled back to Dergan, who frowned. "I don't like it," he said flatly.

"You'll be coming away with something you didn't have this morning . . . and it's better than getting all dirty and banged up in a wrestling match . . . Hmm?"

"All right," Dergan finally said.

"I also agree," said Blaye, less than cheerfully.

"Cow or buck," Dergan snapped.

"I'll decide when I see what's first born."

"And I'm going to brand that buck right now. . . ."

Both men bowed to Shirn, then exited, watching each other suspiciously. Shirn smiled to himself; he never ceased to wonder at the problems his people brought to him.

"How did you do that?" said a small, awed voice.

The old man turned to see Kailyn standing in the cavern doorway. "Ahh, you were spying on us here in the great Court of Mountain Law?"

She laughed and came over to him. "They were ready to strangle each other and you sent them away satisfied. Maybe not happy, but satisfied."

"Simple common sense, my child."

Kailyn's face clouded over. "Why do you call me 'child'?"

"I'm sorry. You're not, are you? You're an adult, and soon to lead your people."

Kailyn looked at the floor. "I'm afraid of that."

"Being an adult, or being a ruler?"

"Both, I guess. I'm afraid they won't accept me."

"They will, if you can wear that crown your father left here. The rest is up to you."

"Is that how it was for you?"

"Yes, I suppose so." He put his arm over her shoulders and guided her over to sit on the soft rug. "But I didn't know what I was doing when I became leader here. I was very young, like you, when my mother died and left the homeland to me."

Kailyn stared, wide-eyed. "How did you learn?"

"By reading, asking questions, watching. I found out what had gone before, what was good, or bad. A good ruler does only what is necessary, with a light touch whenever possible."

"But how will I know what my people want?"

Shirn laughed. "Oh, you'll know. They'll *tell* you. The trick is to know the difference between what they say they want and what they *really* want."

"Teach me," she begged.

"No, Kailyn. If you learn it, you learn it yourself. No one can teach you."

"I don't understand how I can devote my life to declaring that I'm leader of Shad."

"You don't. Your people will declare it, once, by word —then it's up to you to *prove* it, continuously, by virtue and deed."

Kailyn gave the old man a hug and left the cavern.

McCoy was busy fluffing up his sleeping mat when Kailyn found him in a smaller side chamber, off the main grotto. It didn't take a lot of arm-twisting to convince him to go outside for a walk.

The night air was crisp, but here in the sheltered valley there was no sharp wind, and it felt almost warm. Kailyn slipped her hand inside McCoy's and they strolled along the cobblestone road that led to the ascending stone stairs. She confessed her fears to McCoy and told of the chats with Spock and Shirn.

"Did they help you?"

"In some ways, yes—and in some ways, no."

"Well, that sounds conclusive."

She lowered her head and gave a short, rueful laugh. "Oh, Doctor. I'm so confused."

"Hey, we know each other well enough for you to call me Leonard."

That made her smile, and she snuggled closer as they passed a low stone wall overlooking the starlit pastures.

"Tell me what you think," she said.

"About what?"

"Leadership."

McCoy snorted. "What I know about leadership you can fit on the head of a very small pin. I'm one of the world's most religious followers. Somebody tells me what to do, that's good enough for me."

"To quote Leonard McCoy, 'Poppycock!' "

"Spock's a leader."

"He claims he only does what he has to do. Besides,

you always question him before you follow his orders. That doesn't sound like a passive follower to *me*."

"Well," he huffed, "who said anything about being passive."

"I've watched, since we came to the *Enterprise*. The captain and Mr. Spock trust you so much that they always listen to you, even if they didn't ask for your advice. You can change their decisions by what you say—you can lead the leaders."

McCoy gazed up at the black sky and the splash of stars painted across it. "You're pretty perceptive, young lady. I guess I do know a thing or two about the subject, but that's because I've been working for some mighty effective leaders all these years."

"What stands out when you think about them? What makes them special?"

"Understanding and compassion," he answered without a moment's thought. "That's what sets Jim apart from some run-of-the-mill order-giver. He doesn't tell anyone to do anything he wouldn't do himself. He asks a lot, but he also gives a lot. Think you can do that?"

"I . . . I don't know."

"Well, *I* know—and I say you can. There . . . are you any less confused?"

"Not really. Spock talked about delegation and trust, Shirn talked about common sense and listening, and you talk about compassion and understanding." She spread her hands imploringly. "What makes someone a good leader?"

McCoy held her shoulders gently. "All of them. And there's not one of those qualities you don't already have plenty of."

She hugged him tightly, impulsively, then just as abruptly turned and pulled him along. There was snow on this section of the ancient roadway. and a gentle dusting of flakes began falling. drifting to the ground in lazy, slow-motion dances. They both pulled their fleece parkas tighter around themselves.

"I was so afraid I'd feel lost without my father, but I don't."

"You sound surprised."

"I am," she said, in a voice filled with wonder. "Oh, I miss him more than I've ever missed anyone else, and I know I may never see him again in this life. But for the first time, I've accepted it. If he's died I know the gods will take care of him, and he'll be happy with them. And I couldn't have done that without you and Mr. Spock."

"Sure, you could have. You don't give yourself enough credit, Kailyn."

She stopped talking and locked her dark eyes onto his. "You and Mr. Spock are the first men I've ever really known, outside of my father and the servants. I didn't even know your names a few days ago, and now . . . I feel so close to you. You were strangers, and now being with you makes me feel secure and cared-for."

McCoy felt himself blushing. He quickly took her hand; this time, it was his turn to pull her along.

"That's good, and it makes me happy—but you don't know us *that* well."

"Why not?"

"There's a psychological term—crisis syndrome. That's what we're going through. They first noticed it back in the twentieth century. People trapped in lifeboats or tunnel collapses or some life-threatening situation—while they were in it, they felt like they were best friends, brothers and sisters, intimate lovers. But once it was over, they withdrew into their own protective shells again. It was the danger that made them feel so close, and once it'd passed, so did those feelings."

"But I don't want these feelings to pass, Leonard. I . . . I've never felt them before."

"Aww, don't worry—we'll never be strangers to each other again. . . ."

Kailyn leaned on the snowy wall, sniffling, as a tear edged down her cheek. "But I love you."

"You've been reading quite late, Mr. Spock," said Shirn from the doorway of the scroll room. "We need to get an early start in the morn."

"I shall retire shortly. These records have been so fascinating that I lost track of the hour."

Shirn chuckled. "Dr. McCoy said you'd use that word —fascinating. I'm glad you haven't found our history dull."

"Quite the contrary, sir. Have the doctor and Kailyn already gone to sleep?"

Shirn frowned. "I don't know."

The herdsman and Spock went to the sleeping chamber

—it was empty, and Shirn's frown deepened. "Where could they be at this hour?"

"Perhaps they went outside for a walk. Their parkas are gone, and Dr. McCoy is not fond of cave-dwelling."

"If so, we must get them back inside at once," Shirn said gravely. "The night is not safe here."

He led the way, and they hurried through the caves.

# Chapter Eighteen

The stone-paved roadway had ended, and Kailyn and McCoy continued along a path at the base of a high cliff. The smooth wall of rock rose up to blend with the dark sky—it was hard to tell where one ended and the other began. Below them, the steep slope fell away to the valley floor hundreds of feet down. They walked side by side, but not touching.

"But love . . . well, it's not something you can feel in twenty minutes—or even a few days," McCoy said, as soothingly as he could.

"What is it, then?" she asked, trying not to cry.

"It's . . . it's something different to everyone."

"To you?"

He cleared his throat—this was not an easy conversation. "A lot of things. Caring about someone more than I care about myself . . . enjoying someone's company through thick and thin . . . trusting completely . . ."

"I feel all those things about you. But you tell me I don't really love you."

"Aww, Kailyn," he drawled, "I'm not the one for you."

"Why not?"

"I'm just an old country doctor, not a Prince Consort."

But she chose not to listen. Instead, she wrapped her arms around his neck and kissed him. It was not an innocent kiss, and to his own surprise, McCoy returned it. They held each other in a lovers' embrace, and he kissed her hair.

"Kailyn, I'm old enough to be your father."

"But you're not my father," she whispered.

That was true, and despite his protests, he didn't feel like her father at the moment. In fact, he felt things he didn't know were still inside him, things he'd always believed had died with his marriage. Not merely physical desires—they'd never been hard to conjure up. But the desperate longing in his gut to share emotions with someone, to be close and never part—*that* he'd forgotten, misplaced. Could he really be in love with this girl?

There was a soft thump from the path a few yards ahead of them. He glanced up and saw a little lump of snow that hadn't been there a moment ago. Was someone throwing snowballs, someone's idea of a joke? Before he could turn to look around, the silent night was shattered by a screeching roar from above and behind. Fangs and white fur flew at them. McCoy felt pain and hot breath as he fell backward.

Somehow, he'd managed to push Kailyn with all his strength, out of the way. Giant claws slashed at his throat. No place to go but over the cliff. Then he felt searing heat, heard a high-pitched whine, his head spun and he fought the blackout coming on. Suddenly, the incredible weight on his shoulders was gone, the claws and fangs falling away from him. Hands grabbed him—Kailyn's hands—he held them, felt them give way, felt himself fall back. He slipped, hit his head on the ground. Four more hands, strong ones, grasped him, and Spock and Shirn lifted him from the ledge to safety.

McCoy opened his eyes. His entire body hurt. A wave of dizziness washed over him and he felt very nauseous. Spock's was the first face he saw. He moved his tongue over his lips—it felt heavy and soft and like it belonged to someone else.

"Which army marched through my mouth, Spock?"

"I'm pleased to see you've regained consciousness, Doctor."

"What happened? Where am I?"

"You were attacked by a zanigret. You are back in the caves."

McCoy closed his eyes and groaned. "Did I win?"

"Yes. With some assistance. Why were you walking outside? Shirn warned us earlier to remain within the caves during darkness."

"I forgot. Kailyn wanted to . . . Ohmygod, is she okay?"

"Fortunately, she escaped injury. I gave her a sedative and put her to sleep."

McCoy let out a long breath. "You'd make a good nurse, Spock. The last thing I remember is a snowball bein' thrown at us."

"The zanigret's rather ingenious method of hunting is to distract the attention of its prey by throwing a chunk of snow or rock with its prehensile tail, then to pounce from behind."

"Oh. I feel like my back is broken, but of course, if it was, I couldn't feel anything."

"Thank you for that lesson in anatomy and physiology."

"Don't be sarcastic with an injured man. How bad is it?"

"You have minor cuts and bruises."

"That's comforting. Not *comfortable*, mind you . . . but comforting." He managed to sit up—it felt no better, but it felt no worse, either. He noticed Kailyn sleeping soundly across the chamber. Spock must have given her a hefty tranquilizer dose.

"Spock," McCoy said slowly, "Kailyn's in love with me."

The Vulcan raised an eyebrow. "Indeed?"

"Don't act so surprised. I happen to be quite lovable."

"I have never doubted that, Doctor," Spock replied wryly.

"What I want to know is, what should I do about it?" He rubbed the back of his head, and found a knot the size of his fist—or so it felt. He winced, then glanced up at Spock, who seemed unwilling to look him in the eye.

"I . . . am not comfortable discussing such matters, Dr. McCoy."

"I'm not asking for pearls of romantic wisdom from that cold, calculating Vulcan heart. I'm just asking for a logical appraisal, based on that computerlike, unemotional way you have of observing emotional behavior."

The first officer drew his lips into a thin line, and McCoy began to regret having asked him. He'd spent years chiding Spock for his inability to *feel* rather than think, spouting on about how good, old-fashioned emotions were far superior to life governed by logic and equations. At times, he'd brandished the notion like a blackjack, beating Spock over the head with it, rather crudely; on other occasions, he could turn the belief into a sharp tool, wielding it with fine surgical skill, attempting to whittle and slice through the Vulcan shell to the heart beneath.

*All that effort, and here I am turning to him for ice-water advice.*

But this was different. Not merely a private affair of his own heart. He was letting his feelings get in the way of a vital Star Fleet mission. He could not simply regard Kailyn as a young lady of obvious attraction, though she was. Even Kailyn's own wishes had to be submerged for the good of her home planet. *You're a little old to be a star-crossed lover, McCoy.*

Finally, Spock coughed to relieve the silence, though it did nothing to relieve the tension McCoy felt knotting his stomach.

"I am not an authority on this subject, Dr. McCoy—"

"But you're the only thing I've got, so give me an answer."

"Very well. From what I understand about such emotional behavior as this, you have a dilemma."

"I already know that."

"If you do not share Kailyn's feelings, the only way to get her to abandon them is to tell her. The longer you wait, the more difficult it will be to do so." He paused for an extra moment of contemplation. "Clearing the air, so to speak, might relieve her of the burden of confusion over your mutual feelings, enabling her to devote full concentration to the Crown."

"So I should tell her . . ."

"On the other hand, she could react irrationally if she knows that her love for you will remain unrequited. That being the case, your telling her might destroy her ability to control the Crown's crystals."

McCoy scowled. "So I *shouldn't* tell her . . ."

Spock scratched his chin. "A third possibility just occurred to me. She may be so confused now that her mental concentration has already been impaired to a critical point."

"Then it wouldn't matter *what* I do," McCoy said, in total despair. "You're a big help, Spock."

"I assume you are being sarcastic."

McCoy shook his head, mad at himself. "I'm sorry. You

tried. I guess I'll just have to figure this one out for myself."

The next morning dawned bright and clear. McCoy had a restless night of tossing and turning, and he was up with the sun, taking a morning stroll and watching the fine mists burn away from the low-lying pastureland.

In groups of perhaps a score each, the snowsheep were being led out of several yawning caverns and driven down the cobblestones for a day of grazing. Each separate herd was accompanied by four or five of the mountain folk; men, women, and children all pitched in to help, shouting at the animals, tapping the ground with long crooks and prodding the odd recalcitrant sheep to stay in line and follow its leaders.

For the most part, the snowsheep seemed to be placid creatures of habit, following the same route to the fields that their kind had trod for hundreds of years. The same thought applied to the herders. Sheep and shepherds alike seemed genuinely content—*and why shouldn't they be?* thought McCoy. *Their lives are laid out for them by tradition, they're prosperous, well-fed, peaceful;* in the entire time he'd been on Sigma, this was the first place he'd seen where life was filled not with struggle but with simple pleasures. He thought of staying here himself. If the *Enterprise* never came back for them, would it be so awful? *Shangri-la,* he thought again as he watched the herds dwindle in size on their descent from the cave area.

Spock, too, had risen early. He'd gone back to the cavern where the scrolls were kept to record additional chapters. He would never tire of studying the past, piecing together fact and legend to trace a line to the present as it was.

Kailyn was the last to awaken. She washed up in the warm water that flowed from a steaming spring, and was about to look for McCoy when he came in to find her. She smiled radiantly, but his expression was somber.

"What's wrong, Leonard?"

"Oh, nothing. I'm just a little sore from our big-game hunt last night. Last time I go for a walk with *you,* Kailyn."

"Don't say that," she said, and kissed him on the cheek.

"Well . . . how are you feelin' this morning, young lady? All ready for the big hike?"

She shrugged. "I guess I'm frightened. This is what we made the whole trip for, the reason you and Mr. Spock had to go through all this suffering."

"It wasn't what I would've picked for a restful vacation, but we made it, didn't we? It wasn't so terrible."

She closed her eyes. "What if I fail?"

"Don't even think about that."

He held her close, and she rested her cheek on his shoulder. He gritted his teeth; he couldn't tell her—but he *had* to. He couldn't be a distraction to her, nor a false hope. On this day, she would have to face her future alone, without idealized images of love with him to salve the pain if the Covenant and the Crown eluded her.

*It's now or never.* McCoy did not love her, not the way she wanted him to. Though there was much he wasn't certain of, he was sure of that.

"Kailyn, we have to discuss something."

She looked up a him, eyes wide as a child's. "What?"

"We started to get into it last night when that zanigret so rudely interrupted us."

She smiled at the preattack memory. "As I recall, we weren't discussing anything. We were . . ."

She tried to kiss him, but he pulled back and disengaged the embrace. Kailyn's smile died away. "What's wrong?"

He turned his back and began pacing. "Kailyn, I . . ." He sighed and started again. "It can't be like that between us."

"But I've never met anyone like you."

"That's just it. You've hardly had a chance to be out in the world, *any* world. You've got greater things ahead than me."

"I want you to share them with me."

"I can't—and I can't lead you on thinkin' I can."

"But I love you."

"You don't, Kailyn, and you'll know that soon. I care about you, very, very much. I'm so proud of you. You've learned so much in the time we've been in this thing, I feel like I'm watching my own daughter grow up—and that's why I can't give you what you want and need. I'm not the one."

A pair of tears rolled down her cheeks, but she ignored them and refused to cry. "The time we spent together, the things we did, the things we told each other—they didn't mean anything, did they?" Her voice was quiet, almost empty.

"Oh, no . . . they meant a lot, and I wouldn't trade them for anything. But it's not love, not the marrying kind. It is friendship . . . deep friendship and affection."

"You don't have to explain, Dr. McCoy."

"You can still call me Leonard."

"Maybe I'd better not. You're right about one thing— I learned a lot. I learned maybe it's better not to trust anyone or let them get too close."

"Aww, no, Kailyn. Don't—"

"I think you'd better leave me alone now."

He swallowed whatever words were trying to tumble out, along with the urge to give Kailyn a hug. He backed out of the sleeping chamber.

With eyes down, he nearly bumped into Spock in the main grotto.

"Is Kailyn prepared for the journey?"

"I don't know."

"Did you have your discussion with her, Doctor?"

"Yeah. I think maybe I shouldn't have."

"She took it badly?"

McCoy nodded, and felt very much like finding another zanigret to stand under. "Honesty is not always the best policy, Spock . . . especially when you've got lousy timing."

# Chapter Nineteen

Shirn sat on the wall bordering the stone road. Squinting into the morning sunlight, he watched Kailyn come out of the cave. Bundled in a parka that was much too big for her, with her shoulders slumped, she looked tiny and frail.

The old chieftain hoped he'd helped her in some way the night before, though he wondered if he'd really had any right to give advice. While he led a conglomeration of perhaps a dozen clans, she was to rule an entire planet. Shirn often thought of himself as a caretaker, placed in charge of a heritage proven over centuries, tested by time and tempered by the winds.

But the young Princess faced quite another situation—to weave cohesion and order from the tattered threads of a planet ravaged by civil war was something a simple herdsman from the Kinarr valley could only imagine. He wished there were some blueprint he could offer her, a certain path to follow.

There was something about Kailyn that made everyone whom she encountered want to help. Was it the immenseness of the responsibility loaded upon her untested shoulders, or the poignant vulnerability in the way she asked questions and sought to gain strength from those she met? That quality could turn out to be priceless, if it lured others of goodwill to come to her aid. Or, it could be a foreshadowing of disaster if she truly was weak and helpless.

Shirn had chosen two strapping young shepherds from his own clan to guide the expedition up to the hiding place of Stevvin's Crown. The two—Frin and Poder—had been picked for a particular reason: they were big and strong enough to enforce Shirn's ruling that the Crown of Shad be taken only if Kailyn possessed the Power of Times. If she could not clear the crystals, as Shaddan religion demanded, the Crown would stay in its secret place. Frin and Poder would see to that.

With food, blankets, and emergency equipment in their backpacks, they led their Uncle Shirn and the three visitors down the cobblestone road. Ahead lay the trail that twisted over the great mountain, up to where the wind gods kept a watchful and gusty eye on the world below.

Kailyn walked alone in the center of the group, with Spock and Shirn behind her, and McCoy glumly bringing up the rear.

"Keep your head up, Dr. McCoy," said Shirn, "or you'll walk off the side of the mountain. The trail becomes very narrow up higher."

Mostly, they moved on in silence, each lost in private thoughts. Spock found himself wondering what was going through Kailyn's mind. Was she concentrating on mental preparations for dealing with the Crown, or was she lost in the emotional reverberations of her unsuccessful bout with love? For her sake, he hoped the Crown was uppermost, but he knew better; he also knew there was nothing he could do about it. It would be a breach of Vulcan propriety to inquire into her present state of mind and offer help unbidden. Still, he felt this nagging impulse to *impose* aid, whether she wanted it or not. Such action on his part would be clearly unacceptable and he distastefully attributed the impulse to his recent overexposure to McCoy's unbridled emotionalism.

Meanwhile, McCoy's subconscious continued scolding him. *Why couldn't you have kept your big mouth shut for a while longer? Would it have hurt so much? You must be getting old—and senile. Either that, or the older you get, the stupider you get.* Self-flagellation couldn't actually accomplish anything—the damage could not be undone, not in time to help at all. But making himself feel as badly as possible also made him feel just a bit better.

Kailyn herself was a mass of confusion. Fear, bitterness, and rage struggled for preeminence. She was angry at herself for misjudging McCoy's interest in her, and for putting him in such an awkward position. She was furious at him for not loving her, and was torn between a desire for revenge and the awareness that it was a purely childish reaction. She wanted to show how adult she could be, how willing to forgive and forget—but she also wanted to hurt the person who had hurt her . . . or who had caused her to hurt herself . . . or who had *let* her hurt herself. She wasn't sure which. . . .

Fleetingly, she thought of whirling in her tracks, and pushing McCoy over the trail's edge—then throwing herself over after him. How melodramatic.

In truth, she didn't know what she wanted—except peace in her heart, and she had no idea how to find it. Maybe it would come with the Crown.

The Crown. . . . She had seen it, as a very small child, on just a few ceremonial occasions. She tried to recall what it looked like, its shape and size, how it felt in her hands, but she couldn't. All she had were pieces of images, glimpses of a thing of wonder through the eyes of the child she'd been.

What would the Power of Times be like, if she had it? Was it something she'd be able to feel, physically; would it be pleasant, or frightening? Sunlight could soothe or burn; wind could come as a breeze or a gale. Would the Power be double-edged, like those forces of nature? Or would it come forth only before the mind's eye? Would it change her?

*Please, let it change me,* she wished fervently. *Let it make me all the things I'm not: . . . strong . . . wise . . . worldly . . . worthy of being loved.*

But at the same time, she was afraid of being changed by something outside herself. Would the Power invade her like a thing from the night, some creature of evil—was that how the Power worked? Was it a force she would have to battle, and if she won, would she then be accepted as heir to the Covenant? If that was the way, what if she lost? She would not be able to rule . . . and what would be left of *her,* of Kailyn?

No . . . the Power must be a force of goodness and light. It suddenly struck her that in all their years together, all the hours and days spent learning what her father had to teach, he had never given her a clear picture of this Power of Times. Why hadn't he? All at once, she felt betrayed. *How could Father have failed me like that?*

She answered herself—he wouldn't have. If he had been able to show her, in words, what the Power was like, he would have done it. *Even after a lifetime with this odd thing, this Power, as a part of you, you still can't describe it to someone else?*

She sighed aloud—if that were true, then how would she ever know, without doubts, that she had it?

Of course, the Crown would tell her for now, but what about forever?

It was all so elusive. Like love. She glanced back at McCoy, his face a gray mask of sadness. Kailyn felt a compulsion to tell him it was all right not to love her—but it *wasn't* all right. She *wanted* him to love her—didn't she? *Oh, I don't know what I want.* She groaned softly, then turned bright red when Frin, the taller guide, looked back sharply to see if she was in distress. She smiled quickly at him; reassured, he went back to watching the trail.

When the young Kinarri reached a narrowing of the trail, with a stone arch across the path, they stopped, and Shirn stepped to the front. He exchanged a few words with his nephews and took the lead himself. They passed through the arch, which Spock stopped to examine briefly as McCoy looked over his shoulder.

"Fascinating. This is not manmade."

"It looks almost like a doorway."

And indeed it was, for the trail, which had risen only gently for the last hour, suddenly turned steeply upward. What had been a hike became a genuine climb, and McCoy grunted as he tried to keep up. Safety ropes had been looped around everyone's waist, and Spock helped the doctor in a number of places where finger- and toe-holds were next to nonexistent.

Finally, they reached a flat overlook, and Shirn signaled a halt. Thankfully, McCoy flopped to the ground and doubled himself over, trying to catch his breath.

"From here," said Shirn, "I must take Kailyn alone."

"Wait a minute," McCoy wheezed. A coughing fit enveloped him, and Spock leaned over to offer a steadying hand.

"Why are we not able to accompany Kailyn?" Spock asked.

"Because that is what her father requested."

"But we came all this way—" McCoy began.

Kailyn cut him off. "This is our way. My father told me I'd have you with me until the last moments. It's something I have to do on my own." While she spoke, she avoided McCoy's eyes.

He watched helplessly as the safety ropes were detached. Kailyn and Shirn remained linked, and they climbed a steep precipice, disappearing over the top. McCoy staggered to his feet and Poder placed a powerful hand on his arm. *To help me or stop me?* McCoy wondered.

Spock came over to relieve the young guide and eased McCoy down on a flat boulder.

"We just can't let her go like that, Spock."

"We have very little choice."

"Never mind that she needs our support. It's got to be dangerous. Shirn's not exactly a spring chicken. What if something happens to him, or to her? I—"

"I know you are worried, Doctor. I, too, am concerned. Logically, this is not the best method."

McCoy looked searchingly at the Vulcan. Of course, the face revealed nothing; but McCoy believed what he sensed—a texture in the voice he'd only rarely heard, a real warmth. He wanted to thank Spock—but there was nothing worse than an embarrassed Vulcan, so he kept quiet.

This was no easy trail. Kailyn wondered if humanoid footprints had been made here since the Crown was hidden all those years ago. Her fingers and toes ached from gripping cracks and ledges that seemed too small and weak to hold the weight of a person.

"Don't look down," Shirn warned, from above her.

"Should I look up?"

"Only as far as my feet. I'll worry about what's ahead."

"But I—"

Her words were swallowed in a breathless scream as the outcropping under her feet broke away with a sickening crack. Pebbles clattered down the cliff face and Kailyn dangled by the safety rope. The scream stopped as soon as she gulped a mouthful of cold air, and Shirn calmed her quickly.

"I've got you. Don't struggle. Be still, Kailyn."

She felt the rope tighten around her middle. It squeezed tight enough to cause pain, but she remained quiet.

"Reach up with your hands, child. Don't try to pull— just steady yourself. Press gently on that sharp rock. That's the one."

Without extra motion, she did as she was told. The sharp rock was solid.

"All right. Now, put your foot in that crevice."

The foot obeyed, as if by itself. The left foot followed. The rope made her feel secure now, and a moment later, she leaned close to Shirn at the top of what she now realized was a sheer stone face at the very peak of the mountain. And suddenly, the land around them was nearly flat.

Virgin snow carpeted this eerie white world above the clouds. Harsh sunlight flooded straight down, and it was hard to judge distances. She gave her hand to Shirn, and the old man seemed to walk aimlessly. Tagging along like a lost child, Kailyn glanced all around the alien landscape. The rest of this planet had been rugged and dangerous, but not totally unlike Orand or Shad. But the mountaintop was blank, featureless, as if the creators of this world had run out of things to put here. Perhaps they suspected no one would ever come to a place so high and desolate. Or had it been intentional, a respite from the turmoil of nature's children—the wind and rain, the land, the water, the people and animals all jealously fighting for predominance.

But on this summit, there was no sound, no voice, no fang or spear, no footfall save those of Shirn and herself. There was only light, the purest force, the beginning of Creation. . . .

. . . And Iyan, God among Gods, lit the stars, one by one, the Book of Shad recorded. And when they were lit, Iyan was happy. For now in the light of glory, He could make the places and the creatures that would live among them. "I have made the light, given unto the stars. They will burn and die, but in living will create new stars. When one dies, I will light another, and never again will there be darkness unto the Universe." Iyan saw the light and it was good. . . .

*Light,* thought Kailyn, recalling the legend of the holy book.

"We're here," said Shirn.

Kailyn blinked, realizing where she was. Before them was a hump of snow-covered rock, with an opening that angled underground.

"Are you ready?"

Kailyn nodded, and Shirn entered first. She lifted her eyes and gazed at the sun for a last look. Even stars died, but while they lived, they *gave* life. While Kailyn lived, what would she give to the universe, to her world, her people? It was time to find out.

The tunnel wound into the great mountain. Shirn lit the way with one of the lanterns salvaged from the *Galileo.*

"It's warm in here," Kailyn said after a few minutes. "Not what I expected being inside a mountain like this."

"This is a volcano—but don't worry. It hasn't erupted in recorded history. Perhaps it will someday. For now, it just produces heat and hot springs."

A bead of perspiration coursed down Kailyn's brow, and they took their parkas off.

"How far have we gone?" she asked.

"Not very. It seems longer because of the darkness."

A moment later, they came to the tunnel's end—a dome-shaped grotto with moisture dripping from the ceiling and a carpet of moss covering the floor and creeping up the walls. Shirn rested the electro-lantern on a large rock and went directly to a nook in the wall. He withdrew something wrapped in a shimmering metallic cloth and brought it over to Kailyn. She looked at him questioningly.

"Open it, Kailyn."

Mesmerized, she carefully spread the corners of the wrapping, and beheld the Crown of Shad.

It was not spectacularly jewel-encrusted or garish. In its simplicity, it was a classic work of art, and would have been even if it were not a sacred Crown. A simple silver headband, still shiny after all these years waiting at the top of the mountain. It had four crests, one on each side, signifying the four directions and the four gods of Shaddan lore. At the base of the front crest, symbolic of Iyan, God among Gods, were the two crystals of the Covenant.

Five hundreds years of order, peace, and prosperity had rested on the meaning and belief behind those crystals, as the future did now.

The crystals were multifaceted, and each polished surface was pentagonal. Though they were only an inch or so in diameter, the depth of the foggy interiors seemed great, as if each was a window upon some unnamed elsewhere and otherwhen. Kailyn tipped the Crown and the fog swirled, like the snowy confetti inside a liquid-filled children's toy. The fog roiled within the crystals, a smoky mixture of browns and grays.

Kailyn seemed paralyzed, as she stared at the silvery object in her small hands. Everything that had transpired since the departure from Orand raced through her mind, a jumble of events unfolding and meshing together like the shapes in a kaleidoscope. Somehow, the pieces fit, through sweep and drift, to finally lead her to this spot and moment.

"Say your prayer, and put on the Crown, my child."

Kailyn nodded obediently. Then she knelt on the soft green moss and faced—which direction? She'd lost track and she blushed.

"Which way is south?" she asked, for south was where the sun of Shad rose, and the direction of Iyan.

Shirn smiled and turned her to face south. She murmured the prayer her father had taught her many years before, in preparation for this day.

"I pray for guidance, that I may follow the path of the gods, and of my fathers and mothers, that I may be a true daughter of the Covenant, that I may lead our people always in light and never darkness. Thanks be to Iyan, and my father and mother."

Her lips were dry and her throat felt like cotton as she swallowed. Her heart began to pound and her hands trembled ever so slightly as they clutched the Crown at her breast. She wanted Shirn to tell her what to do, but the old herdsman had stepped back into the shadows behind her.

Slowly, she lifted the Crown over her head, her melancholy eyes rising to follow it. Then she lowered it, closer and closer to her hair.

"Dammit, Spock," McCoy railed, "I *knew* we should've gone with them."

He had long since regained his strength and he paced round and round the overlook. The sun, which had been straight overhead when Kailyn and Shirn left for the last leg of the journey, was on the downhill slide toward its evening horizon. Spock sat impassively on the flat rock, while Frin and Poder alternately chatted quietly to each other and stared in boredom out over the adjacent mountains.

"Doctor, we had no choice in the matter. Meanwhile, you have been walking so continuously up here that you will be too exhausted to make the descent."

"Oh, I'll make it all right. This is just training. God knows I've gotten more exercise on this trip than I've had in the last twenty years of my life. But that's not going to get my mind off how mad I am. If I hadn't been at death's door when Shirn took her away, I'd have fought those young bucks myself if I had to—"

Spock abruptly swiveled and looked past McCoy, but the doctor was too busy to notice. He continued berating himself, Shirn, Spock, and the young guides for the whole situation.

"Doctor . . ." said the first officer emphatically.

McCoy finally looked at the Vulcan, then spun around to see Kailyn and Shirn climbing back down the last rocks. He rushed over to greet them, to hug Kailyn—but he stopped short and his ear-to-ear grin faded when the Crown Princess reached bottom. Her face was blank, her eyes red-rimmed. He hadn't seen her like that since her father's medical crisis back aboard the *Enterprise*. Not even his rejection of her love had drained her so thoroughly. He felt chilled, far more than the weather warranted.

"What happened?"

Kailyn looked up at him. New tears filled her eyes. "I failed." She threw herself against McCoy and cried into the soft fur of his parka.

The doctor kept his face close alongside hers. He didn't want anyone to see that he was crying, too.

# Chapter Twenty

Spock and Shirn huddled at the edge of the overlook, and it was clear that the old chieftain was deeply distraught; but at the same time, he was adamant—the Crown of Shad would not be going down the mountain with them.

"I am sorrier than you can ever know, Mr. Spock. I wanted her to succeed, as if she were my own child. But the Power seems beyond her."

"Seems?"

"She was able to clear the crystals slightly, but not completely. I gave her three chances—that's why we were gone so long. I tried to calm her, allay her fears as best I could . . ."

"I am sure you did, but her failure does not then appear to be a conclusive one."

"There is no room for degree in this," Shirn stated sadly. "I swore to King Stevvin eighteen years ago that I would uphold his law."

The trip back down to the herders' plateau was much easier than the ascent, and it was made in a hurry before night could settle and bring out the prowling zani-grets. But it seemed twice as long to McCoy, in his funereal mood. He'd wanted to walk with Kailyn, but she'd asked to be left alone, an outcast—so he followed a few steps behind.

Once they reached the caves, he overruled her protests and ordered her to rest—with a sedative to back him up. He and Spock left her in seclusion and repaired to the scroll room.

"It was all my fault," McCoy said, his face buried in his hands. He sat crumpled on a corner rug, all elbows and knees, like a broken marionette haphazardly discarded by an uncaring puppeteer. "I'm the worst thing that ever happened to that girl, Spock. I should be court-martialed for interfering with the mission."

"Doctor, you are being unnecessarily punitive in your self-appraisal."

"Dammit, call a spade a spade," McCoy said harshly. "I was sent along to help, to care for Kailyn's choriocytosis—"

"Which you did admirably. Or have you forgotten that you saved her life once."

"Saved it for what? So I could mess up her psyche so much that she couldn't handle the test of the Crown?"

"We have no proof that she would have been able to perform any more effectively in any case. We all expressed doubts about her maturity and motivation when we first met her and evaluated her."

"But I thought she'd gotten over all that."

"Perhaps it was only wishful thinking. You humans are prone to it," Spock said gently.

But McCoy was too deep in his own misery to even muster a smile. All he could do was shake his head. "I'm supposed to be a psychiatric specialist. I *saw* what was coming, and I didn't do anything to stop it. I was *warned*. Christine saw it, Jim saw it, even you did—and I yelled at everybody to stay the hell out of my life, that I was a big boy and could take care of myself."

"The mind is not an exact device. It is susceptible to errors in action and perception—"

"And I made every error in the book." He closed his eyes. "All because I was feelin' so damn sorry for myself, because I felt old. Well, everyone gets old. Why am I so pigheaded that I can't deal with it?"

"Kailyn was not in love with you because you felt, as you phrase it, old—she loved you because of what she saw in you."

"Yeah—a damned fool."

"No . . . a caring individual who took a deep interest in her, far beyond the needs of a military mission."

"And look at the price she paid because of me."

"Did she not also gain things of great value?"

"Like what?"

"The respect and affection of people who she had never before met . . . the ability to overcome great obstacles in striving toward a goal—"

"Don't you *understand?*" McCoy cried. "She didn't reach that goal, all because of me. I destroyed not only a young girl's life, but the future of a whole planet. Shad is doomed to more civil war because I had to satisfy my own stupid vanity. If that doesn't deserve a court-martial, I don't know what does. I want you to report that."

Spock fixed McCoy with piercing eyes, forcing the surgeon to look at him. "Star Fleet employs living beings, flesh-and-blood creatures with—"

"All the weaknesses that flesh is heir to," McCoy quoted bitterly.

"Yes. Command expects the best possible performance from its officers—no more, no less. As far as my report is concerned, Doctor, that *is* what you contributed to this mission."

"Then if this is the best I can do, I don't even deserve to be a doctor."

Spock was beginning to understand the human emotion of exasperation. McCoy was so bent on picturing himself as a despicable worm, there seemed no way to fish him from his pool of self-pity.

"I had not decided whether to inform you of this, but since you seem determined to belittle yourself far out of proportion to your—"

"Inform me of what?"

"What Shirn told me on the mountaintop."

Finally, McCoy's attention turned away from his self-directed character assassination.

"What are you talking about, Spock?"

"When Kailyn put the crown on, she did manage to clear the crystals slightly."

"She *deserves* that Crown," McCoy hissed.

Shirn sat on the steps of the main altar, trying to remain calm and steady.

"She did not do what she had to do. Why should she be rewarded for that?"

"Because this is not a normal situation! She's not succeeding to the throne in an orderly way like her father did and the Kings and Queens before him."

"I know that, Dr. McCoy—"

"Then why won't you take it into consideration?"

"Because I can't. This matter isn't up to me."

"It is *now*. If you let her take the Crown, no one would ever know what happened up on that mountain."

"Listen to yourself," Shirn thundered. "Listen to the foolish thing you've said. No one would know? *She* would know. What if I let her take the Crown and she went back to Shad? What if they asked her to demonstrate that she has the Power—when she doesn't? Even worse, what if she *became* Queen and had neither the wisdom nor maturity to lead, nor whatever mystical aid the Power can offer? Think about these things before you ask me to break an oath to Kailyn's father, an oath I swore on this very altar, before his gods and mine."

The Kinarri chieftain was seething, and McCoy knew he had pushed him too far—but it was also too far to apologize. Not now. He turned and left the main cave as quickly as he could, the clicking of his boots on the rocky floor the only sound. It echoed off the ceiling and walls and lingered after McCoy was gone.

The hours crawled by. It would be another day before the *Enterprise* might—*might*—reach Sigma 1212. Meanwhile, another sleepless night lay ahead. *That* McCoy could not face. For now, he seemed to be running out of refuges. Kailyn was still sleeping in the smaller chamber, and Shirn was not likely to desire his company after their confrontation at the altar. Frankly, McCoy didn't want his *own* company. The only companion he hadn't alienated—lately—was Spock.

The Vulcan glanced up from the scroll he'd been taping on his tricorder. McCoy sidled into the room, feeling like a supposedly beneficial insect—the kind no one really wants around but no one wants to swat either.

"Mind if I join you, Spock?"

With a nod from the first officer, he sat on the rug and glanced at the roll of parchment.

"What's that you're reading?"

"Nothing you would find of interest. Simple agricultural records. Besides, I assume you did not come in here to engage in research."

A half-dozen snappy comebacks suggested themselves, but McCoy couldn't even mount a halfhearted effort to fire them off. "You're right," he sighed.

"No other remarks?"

"Nope. You seem to be the last person on Sigma who'll stay in the same room with me, so I'd better not press my luck."

"Is there anything I can do to help?"

"Me? No. But you can help Kailyn. I know she needs somebody to talk to, but I think I eliminated myself from contention. Would you——?"

Spock was already on his feet. "Of course, Doctor. I doubt I could ever replace you as a father confessor, but I shall do my best."

"Thanks, Spock." *For everything.*

But Kailyn was not in the sleeping chamber. Without a word to alarm anyone else, Spock quietly left the caves and ventured outside, phaser in hand and a cautious eye roving in search of trouble.

Fortunately, Kailyn was easy to find, standing at the wall overlooking the dark valley pastures. She neither started nor turned when she heard Spock's voice behind her.

"Why are you outside of the caves? You know of the dangers out here."

"That's why I'm here," she said flatly. "I want to die."

Spock stood beside her. They were away from the cliffs and relatively safe from any animal attacks. Since she appeared more willing to talk under the screen of nighttime darkness than within the confines of the cavern, he made no attempt to get her to go back in. "Do you really want that?"

She kept her eyes focused on some distant star. "What do I have to live for?"

"Why do you wish to forfeit your life at such a young age?"

"Because, at such a young age, I've failed at everything of importance, and disappointed everyone who's ever cared about me or meant anything to me."

"No one has handed down such harsh judgment upon you, Kailyn."

"No one has to. I may be a child, but I'm aware enough to know that I let you and Dr. McCoy down, and Shirn, too. And I've destroyed the dreams my father had for our planet . . . and finally, that means a whole world will suffer because of me."

"Odd. Dr. McCoy lays claim to many of the same failures as you."

At that, she turned, mortified. "He does? Why?"

"He believes he is to blame for your self-described failure today."

"It's my own fault."

"Has it occurred to you that no one is at fault?"

Kailyn stared at him, her whole face a question. "How could it be nobody's fault?"

"No one sabotaged your effort today—not Dr. McCoy, nor yourself. The same events might have transpired regardless of the circumstances. You haven't let anyone down—except perhaps yourself."

She lowered her eyes, but said nothing.

"I assume I still have your attention?"

She nodded, her face still turned down.

"Good. Please understand—this is not a lecture. I have no intention of telling you what to do. But there are certain important factors you should consider and I shall endeavor to point them out. First, you were given a task—an immense task for one so young—with very little preparation."

"But it had to be that way, Mr. Spock."

"I am aware of that, and I am glad you accept that no one was to blame for that unfortunate situation."

Spock paused, and his voice softened, losing its pedantic edge. "Most serious of all, you were forced to face something very complex and mysterious in a new, intensive way."

"What?"

"Yourself." He steeled himself for a task he preferred to avoid—self-revelation. "I understand, better than you can imagine. When I was a boy on Vulcan, I led a childhood very different from most children, as you did."

"Why?"

He was encouraged that she was looking at him now, and asking questions. "Because I am half-human—my mother was from Earth. Though I appear outwardly to be a full-blooded Vulcan, my emotional development was a process of extreme conflict. All Vulcan boys must face the *kahs-wan*, a test of physical stamina and wits that marks the passing from childhood to maturity. For me, the *kahs-*

*wan* ordeal was even more important—it was the time when I had to choose between human and Vulcan life paths. Do you know how different they are?"

"Yes. But why are you telling me this?"

"You and I talked about handicaps last night. Whether I chose to live as an Earth human or as a Vulcan, my hybrid heritage would present me with a handicap of sorts. My mother once told me how much pain it caused her to know that I would never be fully at home on Earth or Vulcan."

"Is that why you became a Star Fleet officer?"

"I suppose it is a major reason."

"It's strange that on a planet where logic is so important, the fact that you were half-human would be a stigma."

"Vulcans do not claim to be infallibly logical. Unfortunately, we do maintain some residual emotional responses. I was a victim of one—a remnant of bigotry."

"But what made it a handicap?"

"My obviously Vulcan appearance would have set me apart on Earth, and my human blood causes urges and impulses that are a constant irritant to a Vulcan. When I allow a human characteristic to come to the fore and be publicly displayed, I may feel that I have failed in my effort to be a Vulcan."

"But you're not a machine. You're bound to have lapses. Nobody's perfect. . . ." Her voice trailed off, and she took a deep breath.

"That was a very mature observation, Kailyn. I had to realize very early in my life that one often fails to measure up to one's own ideals. Once I reached that understanding, I found relative peace."

"Then what's the point of having goals if you don't reach them?"

"Not reaching a goal on a given day does not preclude reaching it tomorrow, or next year."

"But if I don't have the Power today, I . . . I'll never have it," she said in a trembling voice.

"That may be true, but you still have a whole life to live. One failure does not mean all is lost. Let it be motivation to improve, to deliver optimum performance in your next undertaking, whatever it may be—not to give up and quit trying."

Her lower lip quivered and she looked up at him. "Is it all right to hug a Vulcan?"

He nodded formally, and very carefully she put her arms around his shoulders, barely squeezing. He was amused by her caution, as if she were afraid of violating some taboo. After a few moments, he could feel her rapid heartbeat slow down a little. He took her small, cold hand in his own, and they returned to the cave.

McCoy slept because he was exhausted. Spock slept because his bio-feedback told him he needed this night of rest to maintain a peak of efficiency. Kailyn did not sleep.

It was just an old parental reflex, rekindled since Kailyn had been with them. In the middle of the night, McCoy rolled over for a one-eyed bed-check, saw Spock sleeping noiselessly—*and Kailyn's mat empty.*

He sat up like a shot, stumbled out of the bedroll, and shook Spock, who was alert and fully awake in a second. It was clear almost immediately that Kailyn had not simply wandered to another chamber. Her parka was nowhere to be found. The supply pouch was taken, along with a phaser, a vial of holulin, and a hypo.

"She went back up the mountain, Spock—and we've got to go after her."

"I wonder how long ago she departed?"

"At most two hours—that was the last time I woke up and she was still in bed. *Come on.*"

McCoy couldn't get his parka on fast enough. He knew she'd gone back to confront the Crown—and herself—one more time. He also knew she'd had enough of a head start that by the time they caught up, she could already have succeeded—or died.

# Chapter Twenty-one

Kailyn kept the beam from the elctro-lantern sweeping along the trail and up the overhanging cliffs, hoping the light would give pause to any beast contemplating attack. The lower portion of the climb presented little difficulty, but as the altitude increased, so did the winds. She pulled her hood tight around her face; that, and the blowing snow, made visibility next to nothing.

She thought of turning back. She knew she was risking her life, that she might never reach the cave at the top of the mountain. But try as she might, she couldn't accept life without this wild stab at fulfilling a destiny woven so deeply into her soul. She knew that everything Spock had said to her was true and right, but it all paled next to the Crown and the Covenant. She was born to tread that one road out of all the infinite routes possible through time and space. So many had sacrificed pieces of themselves, put their lives on the line so she could find that road—she was the focal point, and the light of five hundred years of succession blinded her to any alternatives. For Kailyn, there was only one choice.

And now, there was also a growing sense of unease, a tightness in her gut. At first, she dismissed it as a fear of the mind, a demon of doubt playing tricks on her. But then the weakness, the tingling, spread. The demon was real all right, and his icy touch stole down her legs and arms.

Kailyn stumbled, catching herself on the edge of the trail, one foot dangling over the side. She tried to remember what McCoy had taught her about choriocytosis, and she matched up the symptoms. Crouching in case she lost her balance again, she wobbled ahead and rolled onto her side under a protective ledge. Her head was spinning, but she saw the chunk of snow fall on the trail a few yards away. Her hand found the phaser pistol and she leaned a few inches forward. The night was shattered by the roar of the zanigret.

She flashed the lantern out, and the beast leaped from above, charging toward her. She squeezed, and the phaser beam hit it square on the chest. The great jaw opened wide, fangs dripping frothy spittle, and it fell flat, as if its legs had been sawed off in an instant. It was dead, no more than fifteen feet away.

Kailyn tried to put the phaser back into her pocket, but it slipped from her hand and buried itself in the snow. She crawled back under the ledge. The white mountain cat seemed to waver as she stared at it—what was happening to it?

*Nothing . . . it's you.* She held her hand up before her face and saw five fingers multiplying first to ten, then fifteen, then more than she could count. They seemed part of someone else's hand, distant and cold. She commanded them to clench, and after an alarming delay, they obeyed, folding into a loose grouping without strength.

*Pass out soon . . . freeze to death . . . another zanigret comes along to eat. Got a few minutes left, then good-bye, Kailyn. Need a shot. . . .*

The voice echoing unevenly in her skull had to be her own, though she fancied it coming from the dead animal glaring at her with eyes wide and fangs outstretched. Was she talking inside her head or outside? *Can't tell.*

*Can't do it, can't do it,* the voice chanted mockingly. *Can't give the shot . . . afraid to. Can't do what you never did before. Can't, can't, can't. . . .*

She shook her head violently, trying to bounce the voice loose from the spot where it had dug its unyielding claws into her brain. But the voice only sang more insistently. She stopped listening. Hands fumbled with the pouch, found the medikit. Her hands? Who else's? Hypo held up before her eyes. Three hypos before her eyes. *One of them must be real,* she thought with a fatalistic shrug.

The hands unbuttoned the parka, then slid aside the clothing underneath. Bare skin, mottled red as soon as the cold hit it. Goose bumps. The hands chose a spot beside her navel and pressed the air-jet tip of the hypo against it.

*Can't do it,* the voice jabbered.

"*Can* do it," Kailyn muttered. With great effort, she pushed the plunger and the device hissed its preset load of holulin into her muscle tissue.

A fainting sensation was replaced by a calming. The whirlwind inside her head receded as the drug did its work. And she let out a long, long breath—one it seemed she'd been holding all her life. A wave of relief washed over her and she felt free and powerful. The hands clutching the hypo once again belonged to her, and . . . Was this an aftereffect of the drug? She didn't care—all that mattered was the strength she felt newly flowing from within. Eagerly, she gathered herself together and stepped out onto the trail again.

The only witness was the dead zanigret, and it watched with unblinking eyes as she went. Fifteen feet from its head, the forgotten phaser pistol lay in the snow.

"Doctor, stop and rest," Spock shouted over the howl of the wind.

"No time," McCoy called back. His foot hit an icy patch and he sprawled backward.

Spock's strong grip lifted him quickly. "Doctor—" he began in a warning tone.

McCoy shook his head. "I'm all right—but she may not be." He peered ahead into the snow pirouetting through the lantern beam. "What's up ahead?"

Warily, they approached a dark mound blocking the path. Spock flashed the light over it—a pile of loose snow glimmered back. "It would seem to be a small avalanche."

He moved the light up to where the slide had begun; it was a smooth line from the cliff above down over the precipice. Spock flipped open the tricorder slung over his shoulder.

"What are you doing?"

"Checking for a body," Spock answered grimly.

McCoy held his breath until Spock closed the scanner. "Anything?"

"Negative. I had not realized these rock and snow formations were so unstable."

"Maybe the wind did it."

"Whatever the cause, we must proceed with extreme caution."

They picked their way through the blockage and moved ahead. Up the trail, McCoy stepped on something soft underneath the falling and blowing snow. His heart skipped a beat and he stumbled back; Spock caught him.

"There's something buried there," he said through ashen lips. He leaned back against the inner wall as Spock knelt to brush away the snow from whatever was lying under it.

The back leg with its vicious talons was all they needed to see, but McCoy's sigh of relief was far from complete—the zanigret carcass only compounded his sense of foreboding as he sidestepped around the beast, then backed away from it. A few yards ahead, he kicked something small and hard, and inhaled suddenly.

"What now, Doctor?"

McCoy bent down and sifted the snow with his foot. He picked up the phaser and handed it to Spock.

"Well," said the Vulcan, "we know she made it this far. This phaser was likely the cause of the zanigret's death."

"Thank the lord for that, but why did she leave it behind?"

"I don't know. Do you think she would have needed a shot by now?"

"Probably."

"What if she did not take it?"

"I don't even want to think about that."

But he did think about it—and the awful ways Kailyn might already have died.

The lantern light flooded the steamy grotto. Kailyn lay back on the moss-covered ground, the parka folded under her head as a pillow. Through closed eyelids, the bright lantern looked like sunlight. The warmth of the air, the sweet smell of the moss, the sounds of trickling water nearby—it all seemed like a summertime dream as she relaxed.

But this was no summer idyll; she was at the top of an arctic volcano, for one purpose. Slowly, she rolled onto her knees, then stood. The Crown was back in its niche, carefully swathed again in the woven metallic cloth. She set it on her parka and unwrapped it. Somehow, it seemed less imposing this time, as if the shine had dulled. She thought of it as a living thing that had put on its best face before, but was not prepared for such a late-night visitor to rouse it from rest.

She straightened up and held the Crown out in front of her. The prayer . . . she murmured it quickly, then held her breath. Facing a glassy pool of water as a mirror, she placed the Crown abruptly on her head. She closed her eyes and concentrated.

The crystals ceased their inner turmoil. Kailyn bent closer to the water and looked—they were clearing. They'd been dark and murky as a fogbound dawn; now, they turned frosty, a steely blue-gray replacing the muddied mist within. Kailyn swayed and sank to her knees; the Crown toppled to the ground. Tears ran down her cheeks as she saw that the crystals had reverted.

Her whole body slumped and she began to cry with deep, heaving sobs. *Motivation to improve,* said a voice, ringing in her ears. Spock's voice. She sat back on her heels and throttled the next sob as it tried to escape her throat. She reached for the Crown, and placed it on her head again. She thought about Spock and McCoy, and the tenacity they'd displayed time and again since the *Galileo* had left the *Enterprise*—how many times she herself would have given up had the choice been hers. And her father, waiting patiently all those years for the tide of fortune to pick them up and sweep them back to Shad and peace. Shirn, and Captain Kirk, steadfast in their duties. Not a single image of the Crown intruded.

A rush of light-headedness hit her. Her breasts rose and fell as she panted for air. *Another shot, another shot,* the shrewish voice taunted again.

She tried to turn and lurch toward the medikit across the grotto. Her legs melted beneath her and she pitched over on her side. The Crown rolled off and she reached for it, dragging it before her eyes.

*The crystals were clear.* The dark haze had given way to a pearly azure and she could see through them. She sat up and gazed in wonder around the cave, at the moss and rock. Everything looked sky-blue through the crystalline lenses. Magically, her breathing became strong and regular. Her heart soared and she cried out triumphantly. *She had won.*

* * *

Orange and pink streaked the indigo sky as the first glimmerings of dawn tinted the Kinarr mountain range. Spock and McCoy hauled themselves up over the last ridge and stood wearily at the top of the world. The wind puffed occasionally, and footprints were still visible under the fresh cover of morning snow.

Following the tracks, they found the opening into the mountain. From light back into darkness, the beam led the way. McCoy prayed they'd find Kailyn sleeping inside, but didn't expect to.

"Oh, my god," he breathed when they entered the dead-end grotto. Kailyn lay motionless on the ground, curled up on her parka. McCoy stepped over and knelt uncertainly.

"Kailyn . . . ?" he whispered.

She turned over, rubbed the sleep from her eyes, and smiled. Then she took the Crown from its cover and ceremoniously set it upon her head. The crystals sparkled clear and blue.

Wordlessly, McCoy hugged her harder than he'd ever hugged anyone in his life.

"Your father would be proud," said Spock.

Kailyn's dewy eyes beckoned him, and at last he was drawn into the embrace.

# Chapter Twenty-two

Shirn paced along the cobblestones beneath a cloud-powdered midmorning sky, his feet tracing the groove worn by years of sheep hooves walking to and from the pastures. A shout from a lookout came down the stone steps, and the old herdsman peered up, shading his eyes against the reflections off the snow. He could discern three people walking slowly down and he came to meet them at the bottom.

"I should have you flogged," he snorted, "but your faces tell me I would be flogging the next Queen of Shad if I did."

Kailyn skipped off the last step and threw her arms around Shirn. The careful climb from the mountaintop had done nothing to quench her euphoria.

"You did a foolish thing going back there yourself," he said reproachfully.

"But is not the nature of leadership to occasionally do things others consider foolhardy?" said Spock.

With a wry smile, Shirn had to nod. "Yes, yes, I suppose so. You must all be tired. You didn't get much sleep last night. Come inside and rest. When you've caught up —we'll tire you out all over again with a celebration all night *tonight*."

He spread his arms and led them toward the caves.

"Two feasts in short order!" cried Shirn, his voice reverberating through the packed eating hall. He hoisted a silvery goblet and everyone did the same. "What a pleasure! Drink, my friends and kin!"

Glasses and cups tipped bottoms up, and trays of freshly prepared food were brought in, dwarfing even the religious celebration of just a couple of nights before.

"You folks sure know how to throw a party," McCoy chuckled, digging in heartily. "I'll miss this when we're back on that dull starship." He sighed. "Spock, do you think the *Enterprise*'ll find us up here?"

"Most likely."

"Too bad . . ."

"Doctor, I have every expectation that by this time tomorrow, we shall be well on our way to Shad."

"And then you'll finally be rid of me," said Kailyn. "No more babysitting."

McCoy grinned like a farmboy playing hooky. "You don't need a babysitter, young lady. You've proven that."

"Weren't you afraid when the zanigret attacked?" asked Shirn seriously.

"If I hadn't been on the verge of a fainting spell, I would have been. It's lucky I wasn't thinking very straight."

"Yeah," McCoy drawled, "but if that cat had jumped you two minutes later, you wouldn't have been able to shoot straight."

"I don't think I *did* shoot straight. How else could I have hit it?"

"Look at this—at her age, and she's already telling tall stories," McCoy said with a laugh.

Echoes of shouting intruded from the main cavern, and Shirn's ears perked up. A moment later, Frin, the young mountain guide, rushed in with a fearful female companion clinging to his hand. He squatted next to the old chieftain and whispered in his ear.

"Uncle, you'd better come out."

"What's going on?"

"Traders from the lowlands have arrived—"

"So deal with them—"

"But they have a slave to trade, Uncle."

"We don't *need* slaves. We—"

"She's making much noise. They refuse to take her back with them. If we don't trade for her, they threaten to slash her throat right here."

Shirn made a disgusted face and Frin helped him to his feet. "Excuse me, my friends. These lowland tribesmen have a way of arriving at just the wrong time to sell us just the wrong thing. Enjoy yourselves and I'll return as soon as I send them on their way, or at least shut them up for the night."

As Shirn and Frin left the dining cave, Spock got up to follow. McCoy grabbed his wrist. "Where are you going?"

"To satisfy my curiosity."

McCoy shrugged, and he and Kailyn wandered after Spock. Out in the large central chamber, the chaotic shouting partly resolved into a growling alien tongue that made McCoy shiver. He gripped Spock's shoulder.

"They're the ones who captured us." He drew back into the shadows and tried to pull Spock and Kailyn with him, but the Vulcan pressed forward. Several Kinarri were on the fringes of the free-for-all, trying to make peace. And in the center, a hoarse female voice roared over all of them.

"You filthy swine! You'll pay for this brutality! You animals . . . putrid scum!"

As Spock ventured closer, he could only see that she was kicking and biting anyone who tried to subdue her.

"My people will come back and burn you to the ground, all of you! We'll torture every last one—you'll dread the day you were born! You can't treat a Klingon this way!"

"A *Klingon?*" exclaimed McCoy.

"Fascinating."

At last, four of the huge hunters, with the help of several Kinarri hands, caught Kera's feet in a rope. They trussed her like a wild boar and threw her to the ground, knocking the wind out of her and forcing her into momentary silence. The old hunter with the wild silver hair stood over her, shaking his head in a mixture of anger and rueful cynicism. It appeared his luck with live merchandise had gotten no better.

A crowd had begun to gather as people poked out of the feast to see what the commotion was. Spock found Shirn off to one side. The chieftain was not happy.

"Why do they bring things like this to our domain?" he lamented. "We've told them time and time again we have no use for—"

"Purchase this slave," said Spock quietly.

Shirn did a double-take. *"Why?"*

"She can be of use to us."

"As a slave?" Shirn's countenance revealed his astonishment.

"No. As a source of information. She is a Klingon, and undoubtedly part of a larger force sent to sabotage our mission, perhaps to kill us and Kailyn and steal the Crown."

"As you wish, Mr. Spock."

Shirn waded back into the crowd to authorize the trade, and Spock, McCoy, and Kailyn slipped back to the feast, avoiding the silver-haired hunter.

"Good," said McCoy. "I'd hate to see a custody fight over us."

For the first time in days, the silver-haired hunter was happy. Not only had he gotten rid of that shrieking, wild-animal female, but he'd finally gotten his shiny-tipped spear. He could hunt better for simple *animal* animals now, and he hoped bad fortune would follow another hunter for some time, keeping slaves as far away from him as the sun was from the moons. . . .

"Your suspicions were right," Shirn said as he took his place on the dinner rug again.

"The hunters were willing to talk to you?" asked Spock.

"Oh, yes, yes. The leader was so happy to get a steel-pointed spear, he would've gladly stayed and talked all night. But their language makes my brain hurt."

"You deal with these people often?" said McCoy.

"They come up now and again, to trade furs and roots and wooden handiwork. We don't have much wood up here, so the trade is useful. We give them sheep wool and meat, and some modern tools we get from interstellar traders that come by."

"What of the Klingon?" said Spock. "How did they capture her?"

"They were out on a morning foray, much like when they found you. She was lost in the forest, dazed. She was so easy to capture, they were all the more shocked when she regained her strength and fought like a cornered zani-gret."

"An apt description."

"She was so beaten and bruised," said McCoy. "Did they do that to her?"

Spock turned an inquiring eyebrow toward him. "Why

are you suddenly concerned with the welfare of a Klingon intelligence agent?"

"It's just that those hunters didn't seem brutal when they had us."

"They don't usually beat their prisoners," said Shirn. "They said they found her that way, and they found the body of a male of her kind, too, along the river."

"Must've gotten caught in one of those killer storms," McCoy mused.

"Along the river," Spock repeated, frowning.

"Is that significant?" asked Shirn.

"That's where *we* came down," said McCoy. "Do you think they found the shuttle wreck?"

"It is probable, since we left the automated emergency beacon on."

McCoy squinted quizzically. "How in blazes did they wind up here in the first place?"

"The only logical conclusion is that we were followed almost from the start."

"You mean since we left the *Enterprise?*" said Kailyn with a shiver. "How could they? This was a secret mission."

"Not so secret as we figured," said McCoy. "We aren't out of the hole yet, are we, Spock?"

"I would assume not. We must consider these possibilities. One, that the Klingons knew about the entire mission somehow, perhaps from an informant close to the King. Two, that this unfortunate Klingon spy team was not operating in a vacuum, that other Klingon support forces must be in the vicinity. Three, that the *Enterprise* is likely to run into further interference when it approaches this planet."

"And four, we can't count on Jim finding us here anymore," McCoy said grimly.

"It is imperative that we remove ourselves from Sigma and attempt to rendezvous with the *Enterprise* in space."

"But how?" asked Kailyn. "We don't have a ship."

"But the Klingons might have," said McCoy quickly.

"That," said Spock, "is our only reasonable opportunity. And if such a ship exists, it would be fairly close to the shuttlecraft."

Kailyn tugged at McCoy's sleeve. "But what if the Klingons were just dropped here by a large ship? What if they didn't land in one?"

"Then we could be in a lot of trouble."

"Shirn," Spock said, "can you guide us back to the low-lands to search for this Klingon vessel?"

"Of course. We can leave first thing in the morning. But what do I do with this slave, this Klingon wild woman?"

"I would like to question her," Spock offered.

"I mean *after* that. I don't want her here, and I don't want to kill her . . ."

"Ship her back to the hunters," McCoy suggested wryly.

Shirn gave him a sour look.

"I believe the good doctor was joking, though I have never quite understood his sense of humor," Spock said. "If you can hold her here for now, when and if we meet the *Enterprise*, we will take her aboard as an espionage prisoner."

"I liked my idea better," McCoy pouted. "You have no sense of poetic justice, Spock."

"I suggest we get plenty of rest tonight," Shirn said, clasping his hands and yawning.

"But what about the celebration?" Kailyn asked, a bit disappointed.

"When we get back to Shad," said McCoy, "there'll be more celebrating than you'll know what to do with."

*If we get back to Shad,* said the ever-worried voice in his head.

Shirn and a party of ten led Spock, McCoy, and Kailyn down to the base slopes of the Kinarr Mountains. It was far easier than their original journey up to the herders' valley two days earlier, since the natives knew the short-est, least arduous route to the lowlands.

In a way, McCoy hated to go. He paused when they reached the level where Sigma's pervasive skirt of clouds swallowed up the sun and all its brightness.

"Y'know, I'd never be able to live on a world where I couldn't see the sun," he said wistfully to Shirn.

"Perhaps that's why our ancestors climbed the moun-tains—they sensed that holy lands should be golden, not gray."

The caravan moved rapidly through the foothills, swinging wide of the valley clans and their hunting grounds. The raging white-water current that had nearly killed Spock now trickled gently within the hollow, wearing its placid prestorm disguise. Spock stopped to consult the maps.

"Our landing point is about one-half mile in that direction," he said, pointing east.

And so it was. They found the scattered remains of the little shuttlecraft, and McCoy felt a lump in his throat. "I don't usually get sentimental over machines, but I feel sorry for the poor thing."

"It reminds me how lucky we are to be alive," said Kailyn.

"There but for the grace of God go I," McCoy said.

"How far can you search with your little box?" asked Shirn, pointing to the tricorder.

"Several miles, depending on what it is we are searching for," Spock said. He activated it, and slowly rotated to cover all directions. As he did, McCoy watched over his shoulder.

"Ahh, yes, today must be our lucky day," McCoy finally said with a broad grin.

The first officer was less certain. "It would seem to be a vessel."

"Where?" said Kailyn.

"One mile due north."

At Shirn's wave, the Kinarri took the lead again. After a while, they reached a humpbacked hill—from the crest, they saw the Klingon scout ship, resting in a forest clearing not far from the stream. McCoy shook his head in amazement.

"I never thought I'd see the day when I'd be happy to lay eyes on a Klingon ship."

"We live in strange times, Doctor," said Spock, walking down the hill.

"Was that a joke, Spock?" he called after him. *From a Vulcan? Couldn't be. . . .*

The Kinarri were eager to explore the newfound oddity, but Spock advised caution. "We do not know definitively that there are no other Klingons awaiting the return of their comrades. Dr. McCoy and I will approach first, with our phasers. I do not want to endanger your people, Shirn. Wait until we signal that the situation is secure."

McCoy swallowed nervously, hefting the phaser and testing his aim with one eye squinting. "Don't shoot until I see the whites of their eyes?"

"Shoot if you see any part of them. On stun. Ready?"

The doctor nodded and they gingerly closed on the quiet ship. It was about the size of a shuttlecraft, though with a smaller passenger compartment. Spock and McCoy crouched behind a low clump of bushes.

"Do we knock?" whispered McCoy.

"A direct though cautious approach seems correct."

With that, Spock slid silently alongside the vessel and flattened himself amidships, next to the closed hatch. McCoy did the same and took a mirror position across the hatch. Spock lifted his eyebrows as a signal, then swiftly reached for the door switch and twisted it. There was a vacuum *whoosh* and the hatch cover retracted. Trigger fingers tensed, they waited.

Then, with a powerful step, Spock vaulted into the scout ship and McCoy followed—but there was nothing to be found, except darkness and ghostly quiet.

"How very thoughtful of the Klingons," Spock said with obvious satisfaction.

"Should we check for a parking ticket?"

"A parking ticket?"

"It's an old Earth joke, Spock. Forget it."

"Please . . . expand my horizons."

McCoy sighed. In all the years he'd known Spock, he'd never gotten over a dread of having to explain colloquialisms. "See, back in the old days when everybody had private motor vehicles, they used to park them wherever they could find a space, including places they weren't allowed. So—"

"Why did they manufacture and sell more vehicles than they had room for?"

"The free-market system—stuff yourself till you choke."

"Highly illogical. But I still fail to understand your reference to—"

"You didn't let me finish. The police gave summonses to violators. They had to pay a fine, or appear in court if they wanted to fight the ticket. When the old Apollo missions went to the moon, they brought these little lunar rover cars with them, and they left them there. When we finally went back to the moon to settle down and build permanent stations, somebody went out and put parking tickets on the rovers."

"Why?"

McCoy rolled his eyes. "Because they'd been parked there for about thirty years."

Spock pursed his lips and McCoy wondered why he always went through with these explanations. "Spock, you're a lousy audience."

The first officer jumped out and waved to Shirn's group on the hilltop.

The Klingon vessel proved to be in good working order, with a considerable amount of fuel left. After a cursory run-through of the control systems, Spock announced that he would have no trouble piloting the ship away from Sigma. The time had come to depart.

"We really appreciate everything you've done to help us," McCoy said to the old herdsman.

Shirn bowed his head. "I was only fulfilling a promise made a long time ago to an honorable man."

"It takes an honorable man to do that," said Spock.

"I'm just happy for you, Kailyn, that my hasty judgment didn't keep you from the Crown."

"You were only doing what my father asked of you. For that, I thank you."

Shirn looked at each of them. His eyes were wet, and he embraced Kailyn, then McCoy, and finally Spock. "May the winds of Kinarr be at your backs, always."

Spock raised his hand in the Vulcan salute. "Live long and prosper, Shirn."

"You take good care of yourself, y'hear?" said McCoy in a husky voice.

Shirn gazed at the young Princess. "You will lead long and well, Kailyn."

"I hope I can do as well as you," she said softly.

Spock turned away first and climbed into the Klingon ship. McCoy came up next, and he gave Kailyn a hand. Shirn stepped back as the door hissed shut. He and his people waited until the rocket engines fired, kicking up a plume of flame and dust. The ship lifted slowly and unsteadily at first. Then it accelerated and whisked up over the hills and woodland. When he could no longer see it or its contrail, Shirn turned and headed for the sunny skies of the holy valley of Kinarr.

# Chapter Twenty-three

"I'd make an awful Klingon," McCoy muttered, hunkered down in the uncomfortable scout-ship seat. "How can they torture their people by making them fly in these tiny match boxes?"

"Perhaps that accounts for Klingons' foul humor, Doctor," said Spock.

"What if there's a Klingon battle cruiser out here somewhere?" Kailyn wondered.

"Don't ask things like that," McCoy snapped. "I'd rather know where the *Enterprise* is."

"That is a valid concern," Spock agreed. "The ship should have arrived here almost twenty-four hours ago."

"Is it possible they left without us?" Kailyn said in a small voice.

"Unlikely. A better probability is that the captain encountered some difficulty relating to Klingon interference. We shall achieve orbit outside the planet's storm belt, and remain for a period of time. If the *Enterprise* does come within sensor range, we will be noticed rather quickly."

"And what if it doesn't get here after a while?" said McCoy.

"When that time comes, we will evaluate our position logically, in light of whatever data we have available."

"Are we within scanning range of Sigma yet?" Kirk asked tightly.

Chekov and Sulu exchanged quick glances, and Kirk noticed. He settled back in the command seat with a wry smile. "I know . . . I just asked you that. Forgive me, Mr. Chekov."

"Yes, sir. We are *almost* in range. All scanners on maximum forward sweep. If there's anything out there, we'll pick it up."

"Very well."

At moments like these, Kirk realized just how trustworthy his crew was, without exception. He'd have to let them do their jobs, and he channeled his nervous energy into tapping on his armrest control panel. *As soon as there's something to report, they'll report it. . . .*

Chekov tensed in his seat, eyes locked onto his readout screen. Kirk sat forward, at the edge of his chair. "Something?"

"A small vessel, sir, at the very limit. Too far off for positive identification."

"Verified, sir," said Sulu. "Moving in high planet orbit."

Kirk swiveled. "Uhura?"

"All channels open for reception, sir. We're hailing on all frequencies. No communication as yet."

"Additional sensor data, Captain," said Chekov.

"Is it the *Galileo?*"

Chekov hesitated just a beat, and Kirk tensed.

"Negative, sir. It's a Klingon scout vessel."

Everyone on the bridge looked quickly at the main viewscreen. The mystery ship was just a shapeless spot against the backdrop of stars and the gray face of Sigma 1212.

"That could explain why they don't want to talk to us," Kirk said grimly. "Sound Yellow Alert."

Uhura punched up the intraship channel as the wall beacon started flashing. "Yellow Alert," said the computer voice over the speakers. "Yellow Alert—stand by for status update."

"Sulu, cut speed for standard orbital entry," said Kirk.

"Another problem, sir," said Sulu. "Several storms in low- and mid-orbit ranges."

"Maximum orbit, then."

"Captain," Chekov broke in, "we have another visitor." He leaned over and switched screen channels. The long, insectlike shape of a Klingon battle cruiser wavered into view.

Chekov's fingers danced across his console. "Deflectors on maximum. Weapons crews standing by, sir."

Kirk sat back and stretched his legs. Waiting had made him edgy, but at least now he knew what he'd been waiting for. The time had arrived for action.

"Go to Red Alert."

The claxon sounded and the bridge lights dimmed to a reddish glow. The computer voice sounded shipwide: "Red Alert—Red Alert—all hands to battle stations!"

"Continuing orbital approach, sir," Sulu said.

"Maintain. Chekov, what's the Klingon doing?"

"The cruiser is also making orbital approach, Captain. But he's aiming for the scout ship."

"Well, they're not going to get away without a damn good explanation. Close on the scout, Sulu. Let's beat 'em to it."

"Captain Kirk," Uhura said sharply, "receiving a signal from the scout vessel. Channel Four-B. It's . . . it's Mr. Spock."

Kirk broke into a surprised grin and stabbed his comm selector. "Spock, you've got a lot of explaining to do—"

"Indeed, Captain," came the reply. "We are all well. You are almost twenty-four hours late . . . very unlike you, sir."

"Okay, okay. We both have a lot of explaining to do. You know there's a Klingon battle cruiser coming to greet you?"

"Affirmative."

"I assume he's expecting to find Klingons aboard. Will he be disappointed?"

"Nobody here but us chickens," said a familiar Georgian drawl.

"Good to hear you, Bones. Stand by for—"

"Captain," Uhura cut in, "Commander Kaidin of the Imperial Cruiser *Nightwing* is demanding an explanation for our presence."

"Tell him to cool his heels. Spock, we'll have you out of there in a minute. Scotty, coordinate with the transporter room and beam our people out of there, on the double. Then stand by for maximum warp."

"Aye, sir."

"Uhura, put the Klingons on main screen."

"Yes, sir."

The cruiser *Nightwing* faded and Kaidin's thundercloud

visage took its place. "Kirk, get your slimy vessel away from our scout ship."

Kirk countered Kaidin's glare with a mirthless smile. "I see you got right to the point, Commander. This is Federation territory. You're here only by authority of the Organian Peace Treaty, which clearly specifies that the . . . ahem . . . visiting vessel must show cause for its presence upon demand. And I'm demanding, *right now*."

"Save your threats, Kirk. Star Fleet cowards never back up words with weapons."

"Captain," Scott whispered, "they're safe and sound in the transporter room—and so's the Crown."

An instant later, Kaidin's studied hostility gave way to surprise as a junior officer entered in near-panic and murmured urgently in the commander's ear. Whatever he was told made Kaidin forget his channel was open to the starship.

*"What?"* he hissed. "How could our agents have vanished from their ship?" The Klingon turned, saw Kirk's face in his viewer, spat a string of curses that covered several languages—and the *Enterprise* viewscreen went abruptly blind.

"Take us out of orbit *now*, gentlemen—warp eight!"

The giant starship heeled over to the right, and the intense force of acceleration pressed the bridge crew deep into their seats. On the screen, the star field became a blur.

"Report," Kirk ordered.

"The Klingon cruiser hasn't even changed course," Sulu said with barely disguised glee.

"They're still trying to figure out who was on that scout ship and what happened to them," Kirk said lightly. "I don't think they'll be bothering us again on this trip. Cut speed to warp five and lay in a nice, straight course to Shad. Scotty, you have the con."

Kirk eased out of his seat and headed for the turbolift.

Kailyn took the news of her father's death stoically, and the formal debriefing went smoothly. The reports could be filed later, as far as Kirk was concerned. The mission was actually still incomplete, and he preferred to allow some time for unwinding on the two-day trip back to Shad. After all, they had a coronation to prepare for.

In fact, the best remedy for all the recent tensions was a long dose of R & R; unfortunately, that wasn't possible just yet. The next best thing was a return to quiet routine, and Captain Kirk so ordered.

For Kailyn, that meant light reading and exercise, mixed in with some special reports of information she would need to know by the time she arrived home.

Spock turned his regular duty shifts, played chess with the newly programmed computer, and began indexing the history scrolls he'd found so absorbing on Sigma.

Down in sick bay, McCoy put his feet up whenever possible—they'd earned the rest—and listened to music with Kailyn as he thought about the sun that had warmed his soul high up in Shirn's mountains. He also resumed as commonplace a job as he could think of—the annual physical exams needed to update crew records. Kirk was next on the list, and he came in at the end of his watch.

"How're you feeling, Jim?"

"Well, I'd say you people gave me a few more gray hairs this last week or so, but other than that and the bags under my eyes from lack of sleep, I'm fine." He stretched back onto the diagnostic bench. McCoy turned it on and the scanners did their work, flashing results on the readout screen.

"Mm-hmm," McCoy mumbled. "Uh-huh . . . mm-hm. Press down on the hand bars."

Kirk made a face. "Bones, why do doctors do that? It's very disconcerting to lie here and listen to you go—"

"Uh-oh."

"*Uh-oh?* For what?"

"You've been hitting the cookie jar while I was gone."

"I have *not*."

"Then why are you ten pounds overweight?"

"*What?* That's impossible."

"Scales don't tell lies, Jim."

"And I *do?*"

"A little white one, maybe." McCoy glanced back at the screen. "Everything else measures up just fine. Heartbeat, respiration, blood pressure, muscle strength. Weight's the only problem."

"I swear I've been following that awful diet you gave me, doing more than my normal exercise . . ."

"Maybe you've been sleepwalking past the food synthesizers. How do I know? Am I my captain's keeper? Maybe you've been *noshing*, as my old Jewish babysitter used to say, and you don't want to admit it to your kindly family doctor for fear he'll draw and quarter you."

"I *swear* . . . wait a minute. Ten pounds is—what?— about one-sixteenth of my normal weight? If I gained that much, wouldn't it show up in some of those other figures —heart rate, muscle strength, *something?* If this thing's supposed to be so accurate—"

"I guess it *would* show up—"

"Ah-*ha*, but it didn't. Ergo, your scale *is* lying."

"Jim, it's not an antique dime-store scale that tells your fortune. It's a computerized sensor system that can detect a hundredth of an ounce—"

"And it has to be calibrated, right?"

"Sure, every so often."

"Then it can also be *mis*calibrated."

"Jim, vanity is not becoming—"

"Check it."

"—in a man of your breeding and character—"

"Bones, check it—"

"—and I don't think we're going to—"

*"Check it,"* Kirk roared.

McCoy snapped a mock salute, leaned behind the machine and opened a small access door.

"Mm-hmm . . . uh-huh . . ."

Kirk rolled his eyes.

"Son of a gun," said McCoy.

"Don't tell me. Let me guess. Might your wonderful device be, oh, ten pounds off normal?"

"When you're right, Jim, you're right."

"I won't even say I told you so."

McCoy marched away from the table to the nearest intercom.

"Hey," Kirk protested, "finish me up."

"I've got to call Chekov before he withers away to skin and bones."

The intercom whistled, and Chekov heard McCoy call his name over the speaker, but he was unable to answer just then. He was dangling from the high rings, fifteen feet off the floor of the gymnastics lounge. Uhura glanced up at him from the balance beam, her left leg arcing gracefully in midair, toe pointed like a ballerina's.

"Want me to get that for you?"

"It would be most helpful." he said tightly.

Stifling a giggle, the lithe communications officer

stepped to the end of the beam, flipped head over heels, and landed on the floor in a perfect dismount.

"Doctor, Chekov is sort of hung up right now," she said seriously as she hit the wall switch. "Any messages?"

"Yeah. Tell him to report to my office first thing, okay?"

"I will."

"McCoy out."

She crossed her arms and adjusted her skintight leotard, which hid nothing—though she was much more voluptuous than the traditional gymnast, there was not a single out-of-place bulge or extra ounce of fat on Uhura's body. "Chekov, if you just *hang* there, it's no exercise at all."

"Just tell me how to get down."

"Oh?" she said innocently. "I thought you knew."

"Don't make little jokes, or I'll fall right on top of you. Tell me."

"Just drop down. The floor's padded enough to—"

He didn't wait for the rest, and he landed with a resounding thud.

Uhura ambled over. Chekov was flat on his back, eyes closed. "That wasn't very graceful," she said. "You'd lose a lot of points."

The office door whisked open and Chekov limped in, still in his sweaty gym suit. McCoy gave him a surprised stare. "Where have you been?"

"Trying to lose ten pounds."

McCoy's head bobbed nervously. "Ahh . . . about those ten pounds . . ."

"What about them?" asked Chekov with the wary eyes of a cat near a dog kennel.

"Well, it seems that, uh . . . I've heard how hard you've been trying to lose them—"

"—and how everything I eat has no calories and less flavor—"

"I don't know how this could've happened. It was only this one table. I guess in all the excitement, somebody just wasn't paying attention . . . I'm really sorry this happened, and believe me, the person responsible will be even sorrier when I get my hands on—"

"Dr. McCoy, what are you talking about?"

McCoy looked at the ceiling. "You . . . um . . . you're not ten pounds overweight."

"Anymore?" Chekov queried cautiously.

"Never were. It was a mistake. You can go back to your old routine."

Chekov slumped into a seat. "I don't believe this," he muttered.

McCoy leaned close. "Would you like to hit me? Would that make you feel better?"

"It would—but I'm too weak from hunger."

# Chapter Twenty-four

The recently recaptured capital buzzed with anticipation of its first coronation in many years—this, the coronation that would preserve the planet.

Fighting between the Loyalists and the Mohd Alliance continued in some outlying provinces, but news of the return of the Crown had had the desired effect—sealing the fissures in the Loyalist Coalition and infusing its armies with the spirit needed to quash the revolt. The war would soon be over.

The Great Hall of the Temple of the Covenant was filled from wall to wall with Shaddans of every age and description. Government ministers stood elbow to elbow with dirt farmers, country priests with cosmopolitan merchants, old women with small children. The giant doors in the rear were thrown open and thousands of pilgrims stood in the plaza listening to the choir sing from the balcony.

A blaze of sacramental candelabra on the wall behind the altar glimmered like heavenly stars. The archpriest, a towering old man resplendent in pure white robes, read from the holy Book of Shad. But in the half-sacred, half-circus atmosphere, at least as many spectators paid their attention—and money—to vendors in the open square, hawking everything from food to royal pennants and religious statues.

Finally, the archpriest turned toward the back of the Great Hall and lifted his arms to the choir balcony high above the inside crowd. The singers soared to a crescendo and suddenly stopped. At that signal, the voices in the temple and out in the plaza lowered to a murmur; then, silence.

"That's amazing," McCoy whispered to Kirk. The senior officers of the *Enterprise* occupied a front pew, close enough to feel the heat of the candles arched over the altar.

The shimmering Crown reposed on a velvet pillow of midnight blue, and the priest regarded it with a fond smile, as if it were a favorite child back with its family after a long separation. The near-complete stillness stretched to minutes, when the priest signaled the choirmaster again. The singers began a melodious hum, bass with a counterpoint melody of sopranos woven in, quiet and delicate as a butterfly at rest.

A crimson drape, reaching from the floor to the ceiling forty feet up, parted and Kailyn stepped regally toward the priest, her hand held by Haim, King Stevvin's trusted First General. Kirk watched the old warrior, now stooped with age but with a strong and steady step as he led the Crown Princess to the center of the pulpit stage. The captain threw quick glances at his officers—Spock, looking incredibly dignified in his dress uniform; Scott, with his jaw set at attention; and McCoy, surreptitiously wiping a proud tear from the corner of his eye, hoping no one would notice. Kirk smiled and shifted his gaze back to the stage.

Kailyn wore a long gown of sky-blue, with golden trim at her breast. Her hair flowed down her back and she stood straight and tall, with the aura of one who knew she was truly where she belonged. The little girl who had confessed so many fears in the garden on Orand had disappeared somewhere between then and now.

The woman who had taken her place knelt before the priest and bowed her head as a symbol of humility. Then she looked straight ahead, a vision of solemn beauty. The priest lifted the Crown slowly, held it high, and lowered it onto her head. There was an absolute hush in the Great Hall.

The crystals glowed, clear and blue in their shining silver setting. Kailyn stood—and the choir broke into a chorus of jubilation.

McCoy poked Kirk in the ribs. "She looked at me, didn't she, Jim?"

"Yeah, Bones, she looked at you."

Outside, the plaza shook to the sounds of tumultuous cheering, and bells pealed near and far. At long last, the war-torn planet of Shad had its new Queen of the Covenant.

The palace hadn't seen a banquet of any kind in almost twenty years. Somehow, a staff had been assembled, and the foyers, the broad staircases of marble and alabaster, and the main rooms had been spit-shined and decorated.

Through the whirl of dancers and revelry, a young, shaggy-haired servant found Kirk, Spock, and McCoy on a veranda overlooking the rest of the capital city. Fireworks exploded across the night sky—the thunder of joyful celebration instead of death.

The starship officers were ushered into an empty sitting room, and the servant left them, closing the door behind him. A side door opened and Kailyn rushed into their arms; McCoy stepped forward and intercepted her, taking her hand delicately in his own. He bent low in a courtly bow and kissed her fingertips.

"Your royal Highness."

Kailyn blushed. "You don't have to call me that."

"I just wanted to see how it sounded," he said grinning. "Well?"

"It sounds just fine."

Then there was an awkward pause, broken first by the new Queen. "There's no way I can ever thank you, all of you. I owe you more than just my life. When . . . when I left Orand, I only knew how to be a frightened child. In a lot of ways, I still am. But you've helped me so much. Knowing you, I've learned how to find strength in myself, how to love, and be loved. . . . Most of all, I've learned how to *keep* learning, as long as I live."

McCoy started to speak, but Kailyn raised her hand.

"No . . . wait. I know our lives have to take different paths now, but I hope they cross again and keep crossing as long as we're all alive." She sniffled, trying to stop the tears before they slipped out, then lowered her head and wiped her eyes. "Not very queenly, I guess."

She took a deep breath. "Well . . . General Haim wants me to meet some people." As quickly as she'd entered, she turned and left, and McCoy thought of the first time she'd come to see him in sick bay—the way she'd darted in and out, afraid she was intruding.

The palace celebration lasted well into the night. Chekov was in the midst of one more pass by the long smorgasbord tables, balancing an overflowing plate with one hand and pouring from a flagon of wine with the other.

"Enjoying yourself, Mr. Chekov?" asked Kirk.

"Paradise to a starving man, Captain," he said, squeezing a thumb into his waistband. "We should come to coronations more often."

"I'll make a note of that. Better eat fast—we'll be beaming up as soon as I can gather the rest of our drunken crew."

"But it seems like we just got here, sir."

Kirk shrugged wistfully. "Got to get back to work sometime."

McCoy and Kailyn danced a lilting waltz, smiling all the while but without a word. Impulsively, she kissed him on the cheek and his smile became a laugh.

"What was that for?" he asked.

"I felt like it. If the Queen can't kiss her dancing partner, then what's the good of being Queen?" Then she added in a conspiratorial whisper: "Are you afraid the Council will think there's something between us?"

"There is. There always will be—and don't you forget it, young lady."

Her eyes brightened—the child within shone through. "Then you will visit me . . . I mean us . . . again?"

He nodded—and felt a tap on his shoulder. He turned to look up at a young Shaddan lieutenant—blond, baby-faced, wearing a chestful of medals. He was at least a head taller than McCoy.

"May I have this dance with her highness?"

McCoy felt a wave of old age coming on, felt stooped and gray—but caught it just in time and straightened up. "Of course . . . son." Before he yielded Kailyn's hand, he murmured: "Would you believe I used to look just like him?"

Now *she* laughed—and McCoy froze that image in his mind.

At the edge of the ballroom floor, he found Spock and Kirk and joined them in a last drink.

"She certainly has grown up," said Kirk.

"She had to, Jim."

"Her father always did what he had to. If she's inherited that instinct, she should be quite a Queen."

"Captain," said Spock formally, "I believe you've found common ground upon which Dr. McCoy and I can fully agree."

"I'd like to make a habit of that, gentlemen," said Kirk.

McCoy shook his head and grinned. "Not on your life, Jim."

# About the Author

HOWARD WEINSTEIN lives on Long Island, New York. He graduated from the University of Connecticut with a degree in communications in 1975. "The Pirates of Orion" episode of the animated *Star Trek* series was his first television script sale, and this novel is his first book. He spends his spare time playing guitar; writing songs; and watching television, seeing movies, and reading books (all to check up on the competition). Among his friends are a large collection of stuffed creatures (who also watch television, see movies, and read books—but not to check up on the competition).